# THE SISTERS GRIMM

# THE S...
# GRI...

10th Anniversary Edition

# ONCE UPON A CRIME

## MICHAEL BUCKLEY

### Pictures by PETER FERGUSON

AMULET BOOKS   NEW YORK

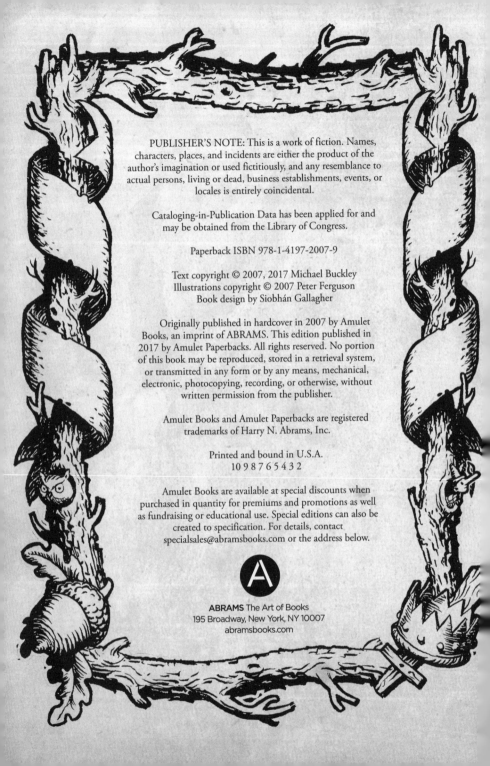

Cataloging-in-Publication Data has been applied for and may be obtained from the Library of Congress.

Paperback ISBN 978-1-4197-2007-9

Printed and bound in U.S.A.
10 9 8 7 6 5 4 3 2

**ABRAMS** The Art of Books
195 Broadway, New York, NY 10007
abramsbooks.com

For my mother,
Wilma Cuvelier

"Get off the streets!" Sabrina cried. "There's a monster coming!"

"Do you people want to get squashed?" Daphne shouted, but New York City pedestrians were used to ignoring screaming lunatics. Daphne turned to Granny Relda with a panicked face. "They won't listen!"

Granny Relda took the girls by the hand. "They will. Run, children!"

The girls shared a nervous glance as they raced down the sidewalk, pushing through the crowd and calling out warnings. Soon, the family came to an intersection and stopped in their tracks. They weren't on the quiet streets of Ferryport Landing anymore; this was the big city. If they tried to cross against the light, a speeding truck or taxi would flatten them for sure. While they waited anxiously, Sabrina took a quick look back, just in time to see the collapse of the entire front of the building they had just fled. A huge leg stepped through the rubble and dust. With a dreadful crash, the gigantic creature freed itself of the store. It lifted one of its enormous, pointed shoes and kicked a taxicab out of the way, sending it slamming into a light pole and then skidding across the intersection, where it crashed into a newspaper delivery truck. The people on the sidewalk let out a collective scream.

"They're paying attention now," Sabrina muttered.

Panicked pedestrians turned en masse and rushed toward Sabrina and her family. Many people were looking back as they ran; a young woman knocked Daphne to the ground in her panic. If the monster didn't kill the Grimms, Sabrina realized, her family would be trampled to death in the sudden riot.

The monster turned its massive head left and right. Its lantern eyes scanned the streets until they fixed on Sabrina.

"I'll get you, my pretty," the monster roared.

# 1

# Four Days Earlier

THE EXPLOSION SHOOK SABRINA GRIMM SO hard she swore she felt her brain do a somersault inside her skull. As she struggled to get her bearings, a noxious black smoke choked her and burned her eyes. Could she escape? No, she was at the mercy of a cold, soulless machine: the family car.

"Isn't anyone worried that this hunk of junk might kill us?" Sabrina yelled, but no one heard her over the chaos. As usual, she was the only person in her family who noticed anything was wrong. Murder plots; horrifying monsters; the shaking, jostling, rattling death trap the family used to get around: Sabrina had her eyes wide open to trouble. She was sure if she didn't stay on her toes her entire family would be dead by nightfall on any given day. They were lucky to have her.

Her grandmother, a kind, sweet lady, was in the front seat, buried in the same book she had been reading for the last two hours. Next to her was the old woman's constant companion: a skinny, grouchy old man named Mr. Canis, who drove the family everywhere. Sharing the backseat with Sabrina was a portly, pink-skinned fellow named Ernest Hamstead, and nestled between them was Daphne, Sabrina's seven-year-old sister, who slumbered peacefully, drooling like a faucet onto Sabrina's coat sleeve. Sabrina gently nudged her sister toward Mr. Hamstead. He grimaced when he noticed the drool and shot Sabrina a look that said, *Thanks for nothing*.

Sabrina pretended not to notice and leaned forward to get her grandmother's attention. Granny Relda set her book down in her lap and turned to Sabrina with a smile. The old woman's face was lined in wrinkles, but her pink cheeks and button nose gave her a youthful appearance. She always wore colorful dresses and matching hats with a sunflower appliqué in the center. Today she was in purple.

"Where are we?" Sabrina shouted.

Her grandmother cupped a hand to her ear to let Sabrina know she hadn't heard the question over the car's terrific racket.

"Are we getting close to the fairy kingdom yet?"

"Oh, I love chili, but I'm afraid it doesn't love me," Granny shouted back.

"No, not chili! The fairy kingdom!" Sabrina cried. "Are we getting close?"

"Why no, I've never kissed a monkey. What an odd question."

Sabrina was about to throw up her hands in defeat when Mr. Canis turned to her. "We are not far," he barked, then turned his gaze back to the road. The old man had better hearing than anyone.

Sabrina sighed with relief. All the rumbling and sputtering would soon be over, and it would all have been worth it to help save Puck. The shivering boy was huddled next to her grandmother, his blond hair matted down and his face drenched in sweat. Sabrina felt a pang of regret. If it weren't for her, he wouldn't have been on death's door at all.

She sat back in her seat just as the car came to a stop at an intersection. She looked out the window. To the left was farmland as far as she could see, to the right a dusty country road leading to a tiny, distant farmhouse. Behind her was her new hometown, Ferryport Landing, and ahead . . . she wasn't sure. A place where Puck could get some help for his injuries, a place her grandmother said was filled with people like him—fairies.

As the car rolled forward, Sabrina lost herself in memories. She'd once been a normal kid living on the Upper East Side of Manhattan, with a mom and a dad, a little sister, and an apartment near Carl Schurz Park. Life was simple and easy and ordinary. Then one day her parents, Henry and Veronica, vanished. The police searched for them, but all they found was their abandoned car and a single clue—a red handprint left in paint on the dashboard.

No one came forward to take care of the girls, so Sabrina and Daphne were dumped into an orphanage and assigned to Minerva Smirt, an ill-tempered caseworker who hated children. She took a special dislike to the Grimm sisters and for almost a year and a half she placed them with foster families who used and abused them. These so-called loving caregivers forced the girls to be their personal maids, pool cleaners, and—once—ditch diggers. More often than not, the families were in it for the state check, but some were just plain crazy.

When Granny Relda finally found the sisters and took them in, Sabrina was sure the old woman was a nutcase, like all the rest. Their father had told them that his mother had died before they were born, so this grandmother had to be an imposter. When the old woman moved the girls to a little town on the Hudson River called Ferryport Landing, miles from civilization, she claimed her neighbors were all fairy-tale characters. She told the girls the mayor was Prince Charming, the Three Little Pigs ran the police department, witches served pancakes at the diner, and ogres delivered the mail. She also claimed that Sabrina and Daphne were the last living descendants of Jacob and Wilhelm, the Brothers Grimm, whose book of fairy tales wasn't fiction but an account of actual events and the beginning of extensive record-keeping by each new generation. Granny said it was the Grimm legacy to investigate any unusual crimes and to keep an eye on the mischief-making fairy-tale folk, also known as Everafters. In a nutshell, the girls were the next in a long line of "fairy-tale detectives."

Sabrina had been sure this "grandmother" had forgotten to take her medication—that is, until a giant came along and kidnapped the old woman. Suddenly, her stories held a lot more weight. After the sisters Grimm rescued her, they agreed to become fairy-tale detectives—Daphne enthusiastically, Sabrina reluctantly—and plunged headfirst into investigating the other freaky felonies of their new hometown.

Daphne loved every minute of their new lives. What seven-year-old wouldn't want to live next door to her favorite bedtime stories? But Sabrina couldn't adjust to the strange characters they encountered. She distrusted the Everafters, and it was no secret that many in the community felt the same way about her family. Most thought the Grimms were meddlers. Others downright despised them. Sabrina really couldn't blame them. After all, the Everafters were trapped in Ferryport Landing because of a two-hundred-year-old magical spell cast by her great-great-great-great-grandfather, Wilhelm Grimm. Ever since, a magical barrier surrounded the town in an invisible bubble that no Everafter could pierce. Wilhelm had been trying to prevent a war, but all the

Everafters, whether good or bad, were trapped. Many of them looked at the Grimms as if they were prison guards.

But the real reason Sabrina didn't trust the Everafters was that red handprint. It was the mark of a secret organization called the Scarlet Hand, and it was popping up all over town. No one knew the identity of its members, or that of the mysterious leader they followed, a shadowy figure known only as the Master.

There was some good news: Henry and Veronica were physically recovered from their kidnappers and at that moment were safe in Granny's home. But, unfortunately, they were under a magic spell of their own—one that kept them from waking up. Uncle Jake was with them now, working hard to find a way to interrupt their seemingly eternal sleep.

Puck had been injured helping to rescue them. He and the Grimm sisters fought the demented Red Riding Hood and her ferocious pet, the Jabberwocky. The monster had ripped Puck's fairy wings off of his back, and now he was dangerously ill. Lucky for everyone, the Grimm family had in its possession an enchanted sword called the Vorpal blade that they used to kill the Jabberwocky. Rumor had it the steel's sharp edge could cut through anything, including the magical barrier. The rumors proved to be true. Mr. Canis used it to cut a hole big enough for the family car to drive through, then he hid the sword in a place where Uncle Jake could find it later in order to store it safely.

Out of the corner of her eye, Sabrina spotted blue-and-red lights flashing behind them.

"What's going on?" Sabrina asked.

"The police are asking us to pull over," Mr. Hamstead said. He and Mr. Canis shared a concerned look, as the old man steered to the side of the road. Canis himself was not well. Lately, he'd been experiencing a change in his appearance that got more and more obvious by the day. Sabrina quietly prayed the officer wouldn't notice.

There was a tap on Mr. Canis's window, and a very angry police officer, wearing a short navy blue coat and sunglasses, peeked inside.

"Do you know why I pulled you over?" he asked.

"Were we speeding?" Mr. Canis asked.

"Speeding? No, I pulled you over because this . . . this tank you're driving is violating at least a hundred different environmental and safety laws. Let me see your driver's license."

Mr. Canis shared a troubled glance with Granny Relda, then turned back to face the policeman. "I'm afraid I don't have one."

Sabrina cringed. This was news to her.

The policeman laughed in disbelief. "You've got to be kidding me. OK, folks, everyone out of the car."

"Officer, I'm sure we can—"

The officer bent down. "Step out of the car," he said sternly.

"OK, let's get out." Hamstead said calmly.

Daphne was still sound asleep, so Sabrina shook the little girl until she opened her eyes.

"Whazzabigidea?" Daphne grumbled.

"Get up, we're going to jail," Sabrina said, helping her up.

They were stopped on a bridge, and the wind coming off the water below was brutal. Cars and trucks whizzed by, kicking up even more wind. The cold air chilled Sabrina to the bone. It was a terrible day, and the dark clouds hanging in the sky warned that it was only going to get worse. "Officer, if I could be of any assistance," Mr. Hamstead said as he tugged his pants up over his belly, "I happen to be the former sheriff of Ferryport Landing, and—"

"Where?"

"Ferryport Landing. It's about two hours north."

"Well, as a former sheriff you should know it's against the law to ride around with someone who doesn't have a driver's license, let alone someone who is driving a toxic death wagon like this one." The policeman poked his head back into the car and spotted Puck.

"Who's the kid?"

"He's my grandson, and he's not feeling very well. We're taking him to a doctor," Granny said.

"Not in this thing, lady," the policeman said. "I'm impounding this vehicle for the good of humanity. I'll call an ambulance and have him taken to New York–Presbyterian Hospital."

He barked an order into his walkie-talkie as he eyed the family suspiciously.

"If Puck is sent to a hospital, they're going to discover he's not human," Sabrina whispered to Granny Relda.

"The boy needs a special kind of doctor," Relda said to the cop.

"And the devil needs a glass of ice water," the officer snapped back. "You should be worrying about yourself. You're going to be lucky if you don't spend the night in jail. Do any of you have identification?"

"Of course," Granny Relda said as she reached into her handbag. "It's right here, somewhere."

But the police officer wasn't focused on the old woman. His eyes were glued on Mr. Canis and the big brown tail that had slipped out of the back of the old man's pants. The cop studied it for a moment, unsure of what it was, and then circled Mr. Canis to get a better look. Canis had suddenly grown several inches taller, and fangs were starting to pop out of his mouth.

"What's your story, buddy?" the policeman asked. "Are you going to a costume party or something?"

Canis's expression was nervous and angry. It was the same look he got when he struggled with his self-control.

"Stay calm," Sabrina whispered to Mr. Canis, but he didn't seem to hear her. A change was coming over him. His nose morphed into a hairy snout, and fur grew on his neck and hands. His body expanded, filling out the oversized suit he always wore. Black talons crept from the tips of his fingers. He was changing into the monster that lived inside him—the Big Bad Wolf.

The cop stood bewildered for a moment, then reached for his weapon.

"What are you?" he cried.

"Oh, here it is," Granny said as she pulled her hand from inside her purse, opened her fist, and blew a puff of pink dust into the cop's terrified face. He froze, and a look of befuddlement replaced his fear. His eyes went glassy, and his jaw went slack.

"You know, some days, being a policeman can be downright boring," Granny said as she placed a calming hand on the officer's shoulder.

"You're telling me," he said in a drowsy voice.

"Like today. Nothing interesting happened at all. You didn't even hand out a single speeding ticket."

"Yeah, today was real dull."

"Still, it was a nice enough day. In fact, you had a great afternoon out on patrol," Granny said.

"I did?" the officer said. "Yeah, I did."

"Thanks for your help, Officer, but we don't want to keep you any longer."

"I should be going," he said. Moments later, he hopped into his squad car and drove away.

"Lucky I brought the forgetful dust," Granny said. She rested the same calming hand on Mr. Canis's shoulder, and his savage transformation stopped, then slowly reversed, though the tail and enormous height didn't go away.

"Relda, I am sorry," he said. "Any little thing seems to set me off these days."

"No harm done," the old woman said. "But for the rest of this trip I suggest you hide your tail."

The old man nodded and did his best to tuck it into the back of his trousers.

"Wait a minute!" Sabrina exclaimed as she watched the squad car disappearing in the distance. On the back bumper, painted in bright white paint, were the letters NYPD. "That guy was a New York City cop!"

"Well, of course he was," Granny said as she pointed beyond the side of the bridge. Massive buildings reached skyward, as if competing for heaven's attention. Airplanes and helicopters flew above them.

Daphne squinted at the sparkling metropolis. One building stood taller than those around it, tapering at the top into a fine silver point. She grabbed her older sister's arm and pointed at it.

"That's the Empire State Building!" she cried, quickly placing the palm of her hand into her mouth and biting down on it. It was one of Daphne's many quirks—the one that signaled that she was happy and excited. "We're home!"

Sabrina's throat tightened as she fought back happy tears. "We're in New York City," she whispered.

The girls jumped up and down, chanting the sentence over and over, louder and louder.

Mr. Hamstead approached the bridge railing to take in the view. The girls noticed his eyes welling with tears.

Daphne rushed to his side and wrapped him up in a hug.

"Don't cry, Mr. Hamstead. You'll make me cry."

"I never thought I'd see this place," he said. "I've been trapped in Ferryport Landing for a long time. Wolf, you should see this."

Mr. Canis joined him at the rail and gazed out at the marvelous city.

"Look at what we've missed," Hamstead said.

The two men stood in silence. The significance of the moment became clear to Sabrina. The whole world had kept spinning while the Everafters were stuck in Ferryport Landing. Cities had risen, diseases had been cured, men had walked on the moon, and Canis and Hamstead had missed it all.

"You're going to love New York!" Daphne squealed. "This city is the best! There is so much to do and see and eat! Oh, I can almost smell the hot dogs from here."

"Hot dogs!" Hamstead cried as his nose morphed into a runny pink snout. Hamstead rarely slipped out of his human form, but when he got very excited his true identity as one of the Three Little Pigs was revealed.

"What did I say?" Daphne whispered to Sabrina.

"Hot dogs are made from pigs," Sabrina whispered back.

Daphne cringed. "I mean, uh, I would never, uh, eat a hot dog, you know . . . they're . . . uh, gross. What I meant to say was pepperoni pizza!"

The little girl looked at Sabrina for reassurance, but Sabrina couldn't give it to her. "Pepperoni, too."

"It is?"

Sabrina nodded.

Daphne cringed again. "I mean broccoli. There's nothing like walking around the city munching on a big ol' head of broccoli."

"Oh yeah, New York is famous for its broccoli," Sabrina said.

Daphne stuck her tongue out at her sister.

"Wait? Why are we here? I thought we were going to save Puck," Daphne said.

"We are, *liebling*. The fairy kingdom is in New York City," Granny Relda replied.

"What?" Sabrina felt her face grow hot. The ground seemed to shift, and she fell forward. For a moment there was nothing but blackness, and then she was on the ground looking up at her family.

"*Liebling*, are you OK?" her grandmother asked. Mr. Canis lifted Sabrina back onto her feet, but the girl still felt dizzy and slightly nauseated. "You must have fainted."

"You didn't tell us there were Everafters in the city!" Sabrina said as she struggled to stand on her own. "I thought they were all back in Ferryport Landing."

Granny frowned. "Sabrina, the Everafters had been in America for almost twenty years before the magical barrier was constructed. Some of them moved to other cities."

"How many?" Sabrina demanded.

"Cities? Why, heavens, I couldn't begin to guess," Granny Relda said.

"No, Everafters. How many live here?" The idea of her hometown having its own secret Everafter community was revolting to her. The world only worked if all the crazy stuff surrounding her family occurred in one place—Ferryport Landing!

"I don't know, Sabrina," the old woman replied. "The family logs didn't track who left town, only those who stayed."

"It could be hundreds," Hamstead said. "Not to mention all the Everafters who came to America on their own, later. It's really hard to say."

Tears gushed out of Sabrina's eyes and froze on her cheeks. She prided herself on being strong, but she couldn't help it. This was a shock. Sabrina had always planned that she and her sister would return to the Big Apple once their parents were rescued. She'd assumed they would all resume their old lives, away from fairies and witches and talking animals. Now she knew there was no escape from them.

"Sabrina, what's the matter?" Daphne asked.

She said nothing. Instead, she turned away from her family and stared out at the city skyline. The initial joy at seeing her home was spoiled.

"It must be all the traveling," Granny said, rubbing Sabrina's back affectionately. "You girls are hungry and exhausted. We need to get you something to eat. Maybe some hot soup would help."

There was an uncomfortable silence among the group until Mr. Canis spoke. "First we must find Puck's people. Where is this fairy kingdom?"

Granny sighed. "Unfortunately, the family journals are also a little thin on New York's Everafter community. I do know it's hidden somewhere in the city." She fished into her handbag and pulled out an envelope with some writing on it. "All I have to go on is this letter from an old friend."

Daphne took the letter and read it aloud, stumbling over some of the words.

*Mrs. Grimm,*

*I'm sorry for your loss. Basil was like a father to me. It breaks my heart that I can't be there for you and your sons, worse because I know I am partially to blame for this tragedy. I hope you know that Jacob and I never believed my escape from Ferryport Landing would bring anyone harm. I hope you can find it in your heart to forgive us. I've found a group of Everafters living in a kingdom called the Greenery hidden in the Big Apple. I've been invited to stay there until I am settled. Their leader, King Oberon, and his wife, Queen Titania, are . . . well, I'm sure you've heard the rumors. Once I've found work and made a little money, I plan to travel and see this big world for myself. Until then, if you are ever in New York City, drop by the park and tell Hans Christian Andersen a knock-knock joke.*

*Love,*

*G*

"Who's G?" Daphne asked.

"An old friend of your father's," Granny said. Sabrina and Daphne shared a knowing look. They knew their father had once been in love with an Everafter before he met their mother, though everyone was tight-lipped about her identity.

"Can't we call this old friend and get another clue?" Sabrina asked.

"Perhaps one that makes sense," Canis said.

"Is there anything else in the envelope?" Daphne asked. Granny Relda looked inside. It was empty.

"I'm afraid the note is all we have to go on," the old woman replied.

"Well, let's go find Hans Christian Andersen," Daphne said.

Granny shook her head. "Daphne, Andersen wasn't an Everafter. He was a writer and detective, just like Jacob and Wilhelm. He died a long time ago."

"You know that, silly," Sabrina said. "We read it on his statue in Central Park."

"There's a statue of Hans Christian Andersen in Central Park?" Granny asked. "Sabrina, you're a genius. Can you take us there?"

Sabrina nodded reluctantly. "What good is a statue going to do us?"

Granny shrugged. "I don't have the foggiest, but it's a place to start."

Minutes later they were over the bridge and cruising through the city's grid of streets and avenues. Daphne gawked at the passing sights, pointing out her father's favorite diner and the playground their mother used to take them to on Sunday afternoons. Sabrina wanted to look out the window, too, but everything seemed ruined. There were few people who would describe New York City as normal, but now that Sabrina knew Everafters were crawling all over it, it seemed tainted, ugly.

Granny turned in her seat and handed the book she'd been reading to Sabrina.

"You and Daphne should probably read this," she said. "It's going to tell you everything you need to know about the fairy folk."

Sabrina glanced down at the book. It was a play by William Shakespeare, entitled *A Midsummer Night's Dream*.

Daphne snatched it from Sabrina and flipped through the pages. "What language is this?" she asked.

"It's English," Granny said. "Early Modern English. If you have any questions about words, just let me know."

The book was a nice distraction. Traffic was especially bad that afternoon. Christmas was only days away, and shoppers rushed into the streets carrying huge bags, slowing the family's progress dramatically. But they eventually made their way southward through the city, and after much searching, Mr. Canis found a parking spot a few blocks from Central Park. The family bundled Puck up in as many blankets as possible and trudged up the snowy, walled path until they found an entrance. Sabrina knew the park like the back of her hand, so she led them down a path that twisted and turned until they came to a man-made pond surrounded by benches. In the summertime, the boat basin was the home of miniature-boat enthusiasts who guided their tiny ships across its mirrorlike surface. Sabrina's mother had loved this part of the park. Veronica brought the girls there on many weekends, and they spent hours eating ice cream and people-watching.

"Are you sure this is the place?" Mr. Hamstead asked.

Sabrina nodded and pointed across the pond. There sat a bronze statue of Andersen himself, dressed in a suit, tie, and top hat. He was looking down at his most famous story character, the ugly duckling, though Sabrina now wondered whether the duck was fiction or a real, flesh-and-blood animal.

"I think this 'G' is playing games with us, Relda," Mr. Canis snarled as they approached the statue.

Granny Relda reread the letter aloud. "It says we're supposed to tell a knock-knock joke to Andersen."

Canis grumbled. "What is a knock-knock joke?"

"You don't know what a knock-knock joke is?" Daphne asked in disbelief.

"He doesn't do jokes," Hamstead said.

"Well, it goes like this. Knock, knock?" Daphne said, playfully tapping the statue with her knuckles.

Mr. Canis said nothing.

"You're supposed to say 'Who's there?'"

"Why?"

"You just do," the little girl said.

Mr. Canis took a deep, impatient breath. "Who's there?"

"Cows go."

Again, Canis was confused.

"You're supposed to say, 'Cows go who?'" Granny explained.

"Fine!" Canis snapped. "Cows go who?"

"No, they don't," Daphne said. "Cows go moo."

Hamstead snorted with laughter, and Granny giggled, but Canis flashed them both an angry look and they stopped.

"You're not going to get much of a laugh from this statue," Sabrina said, rubbing her hand across the figure's bronzed head.

"Well, it can't hurt to try," Granny said as she stepped in front of the statue. "Knock, knock?"

Unfortunately, nothing happened.

"Maybe we need to be louder?" Hamstead offered, then shouted the words as loud as he could. A man on a nearby bench watched them with curiosity. He mumbled "freaks," then got up and staggered away.

"Well, this is real fun," Sabrina grumbled. "Anybody else have an idea before we all end up in straitjackets?"

"Wait. Where's Daphne?" Granny asked.

Sabrina scanned the pond, but her sister was nowhere in sight. "Daphne!" she shouted, as a nervous pain bubbled her belly. She should have been paying attention to her sister. Daphne was her responsibility.

"She was standing right here!" Hamstead cried.

"I do not smell the child," Mr. Canis said as he sniffed the cool air.

Suddenly, Granny smiled and set her hand on the statue. "Let's try this again. Knock, knock?" she said, and in a blink she vanished into thin air.

"I think we've found the front door," Mr. Hamstead said, placing his hand on the statue as well. Canis joined him, shifting Puck in his arms to free a hand. Together the men said the magic words, and they disappeared, too, leaving Sabrina alone. She looked into Andersen's face, took a deep breath, and secretly prayed that her family was safe.

*Knowing my luck, I'll end up in the belly of a monster that enjoys goofy kids' jokes,* she thought.

She reluctantly took a deep breath, put one hand on the statue, and whispered, "Knock, knock?"

The statue's head turned to her, flashed a big smile, and boomed, "Who's there?"

# 2

THE WORLD WENT FUZZY, AS IF SABRINA WERE looking at wavy lines on an old television. Just as quickly, her vision cleared and she found herself outside a restaurant. A neon sign above the door read THE GOLDEN EGG, and Sabrina heard music and laughter coming from within. Her family was nowhere to be seen, so Sabrina guessed they had gone inside to get out of the cold. Before she could do the same, two chubby men appeared in the doorway. Each had big pink wings like Puck's, though the men had hard faces and were much older. One wore a burgundy tracksuit, the other a pinstriped blazer and slacks. They tossed a short, naked man out into the snow.

"How many times have we told you, Emperor? No shoes. No shirt. No service," the fairy in the tracksuit growled. "That means pants!"

"And underwear! This is a respectable establishment," the other fairy added. He resembled a bulldog, with hanging jowls and droopy eyes.

"I am fully dressed!" the Emperor declared. His voice was slurred, and he smelled like liquor. "You are just too stupid to see my clothes."

"You're banned until you learn to obey the dress code!" bulldog-face grunted. He and his partner turned and went back into the bar, leaving the naked man lying in the snow. The man stayed put for a few moments until finally crawling to his feet and stomping away. Sabrina could still hear him cursing as he disappeared.

"That just scarred me for life," she mumbled to herself, then pushed the tavern door open and went inside.

The Golden Egg was a large, wood-paneled supper club with a long oak bar and a roaring fireplace. It had a tin ceiling and smelled like steak and potatoes. Tables were scattered about with roughly two dozen people of all shapes and sizes sitting around them. An ogre played cards with a centaur, a princess talked quietly with elves, and a couple of men who seemed to be part human and part crow were arguing about politics. Other folks were hunkered over tall, frothy mugs at the bar, served by a dark-skinned woman. At the back of the room an enormous man with yellow eyes played a grand piano. Maybe it was just the heat from the fireplace, but the Golden Egg was making Sabrina slightly ill. She felt as if she had walked into the pages of a bedtime story.

She scanned the room and quickly spotted her friends and family standing near the bar. She pushed through the crowd, almost tripping over a hedgehog riding a chicken before she got to them.

"Uh, where are we?" she asked when she joined the others.

"You're in the Golden Egg, honey," the bartender said as she washed glasses. She was pear shaped, with an apron wrapped around her waist. Her warm smile helped Sabrina's stomach relax a little. "We don't serve minors, but I suspect I could find a bottle of soda or two."

"Do you own this place?" Hamstead asked over the bar chatter.

"I'm more of a partner. People call me Momma. Haven't seen you in here before. New in town?"

"We're looking for the fairy kingdom," Granny Relda said.

Momma laughed. "You've found it, lady. What's left of it, anyway."

"This is the fairy kingdom?" Daphne cried.

"Locals call it the Greenery," Momma said.

"Hey!" a voice said from below. Sabrina glanced down at her feet and nearly shrieked. Looking back at her was a walking, talking gingerbread man no more than three inches high. "Watch where you're stepping, kid!"

Sabrina jumped back in horror. In the past three months, she had talked to a lot of things that weren't supposed to be able to talk back, but none of them were baked goods.

"What are you looking at?" the gingerbread man continued. "Didn't anyone tell you it's rude to stare?"

"She's sorry," Daphne offered. "It's not every day you get to talk to a cookie, you know."

The gingerbread man's brown body suddenly turned red, and his icing face crinkled in anger. "Cookie! Watch who you're calling a cookie, kid! Cookies are round. Do I look like I'm round?"

Daphne ducked behind Sabrina.

"Relax! She didn't mean to offend you," Sabrina said, finally pulling herself together. As she turned to calm her sister, she felt something hard bounce off the back of her head. She whipped around and found the gingerbread man pulling a gumdrop off his chest. There was one already missing—one she was sure was now lodged in her hair.

"I bet you thought we were all sweet, too, huh?"

"Did you just throw something at me?" Sabrina demanded, quickly regaining her wits.

"Yeah! What are you going to do about it, meat person?" the little baked man taunted.

"Throw another gumdrop at me and I'll bite your head off, dough boy," Sabrina hissed. Granny was trying to pull her away when the second gumdrop bounced off of Sabrina's nose. "That's it! Bartender, give me the biggest glass of milk you've got!"

The gingerbread man kicked Sabrina in the ankle. Despite his

size, it hurt, and she reached down to grab him. The little man darted away and ran through the bar.

"You can't catch me, stupid meat person!" he taunted.

"Girls, leave him alone," Granny said.

"He started it," Sabrina said.

"Sorry, kid," Momma said from behind the bar. "That guy is hard to swallow."

The patrons at the bar let out a groan. Momma giggled at her own joke. "I got a million of them," she said.

"Enough! We have an injured fairy with us," Mr. Canis said impatiently. "Can you help?"

Momma pointed to a pair of double doors at the back of the bar. A hulking guard stood on either side. "Take him to the boss. He'll know what to do."

Granny Relda thanked Momma and led the family to the doors. The guards were so big they were nearly popping out of their suits. They wore dark sunglasses even though the bar was dimly lit.

"Whaddya want?" one of them snapped.

"We need to see the boss," Granny Relda said.

"Sorry, lady," the other one said. "The boss is busy."

"Listen," Mr. Hamstead said, "we were told to come here."

The guards looked at each other and then clenched their fists.

"And we're tellin' ya to leave," the first one said as he cracked his knuckles.

"We have a fairy here who needs medical attention," Canis growled.

The guard pulled the blanket away from Puck's head, then frowned.

"Not this one. Absolutely not," he grunted.

"What?" Sabrina cried. "Why?"

"This is Prince Puck. He's *liosta dubh*," the second snarled.

"What does that mean?" Daphne asked.

Sabrina shrugged. She usually knew the words Daphne asked about, but she'd never heard *liosta dubh* before.

"It means he is unwelcome," the first guard snapped.

"If he doesn't get help, he'll die," Mr. Canis barked.

"None of my concern. Now move along, geezer," the second guard said, giving Canis a rough shove.

"Pig, take the boy," the old man said calmly. Hamstead took Puck into his arms. Sabrina watched the change come over Canis for the second time that day.

Granny Relda stepped over and rested her calming hand on his shoulder. "Old friend, I'm sure there is another way to—"

This time, Canis didn't seem to hear her. Before the old woman could finish her sentence, he filled out his suit with fur and muscle. His eyes turned icy blue, and he grew a foot taller, towering over the guards.

"Listen, grandpa," the second guard said with a yawn. "Your

little changing act don't impress me none. Move along before things get ugly."

"Oh, they're already ugly," Canis snarled. He backhanded the man, sending him sailing across the tavern. The guard smashed against a mirror behind the bar. Bottles and glasses crashed down on his head. Suddenly, the music and chatter stopped and all eyes turned to Sabrina and her family and friends.

Much to her surprise, the remaining guard didn't run for his life. Instead, he went through a disturbing transformation of his own. His body doubled in size and his skin turned a muddy green. He grew pointy ears like a bat and his lower jaw jutted out past his nose. Two gnarled tusks like those on a saber-toothed tiger jutted out of his mouth, and his eyes turned the color of blood.

"Goblins!" Hamstead cried.

The guard snatched up a knotty club leaning in the corner, and he swung into Mr. Canis's chest as if he were trying to hit a home run. The blow was like a tiny annoyance to the wolf, and he snatched the weapon away, crushing it into splinters. He seized the guard around the neck and lifted him off the ground with one hand.

"The boss will kill you," the first guard threatened from behind the bar as he sprang to his feet. He was already changing into a beast as gruesome as his partner.

"I'd like to see him try," Canis said with a wicked laugh. "Do you think he can stand up to the Big Bad Wolf?"

A chill raced up Sabrina's back. Mr. Canis was certainly losing control of himself if he was now referring to himself as the monster he so often tried to constrain.

"I smell your fear, darkling," he continued. "It's delicious."

"What is going on here?" bellowed a voice. Four children appeared from nowhere and surrounded the family. They seemed roughly Sabrina's age, but there was something otherworldly about them: porcelain skin, blond hair, eyes as shiny as jewels. They wore jeans, black boots, and leather jackets, and they would have looked like normal kids if it weren't for their pink wings and the crossbows they leveled at Mr. Canis's head. The leader of the group stepped forward. He had a head of shaggy hair, like another fairy Sabrina knew well. In fact, he looked a lot like Puck. "They are attempting to see the boss," the second goblin croaked.

"Which will be more likely if he lets you go," the fairy said, eyeing Canis patiently.

Granny set a hand on Mr. Canis's shoulder. "Old friend," she said softly, and this time it calmed him. He set the goblin back on his feet, then shrank to his familiar form. For a moment, he glanced around the room as if he wasn't sure where he was, then looked down at his left hand with a confused expression. It had not changed back with the rest of his body. It was still covered in thick brown fur and sharp black talons.

"Why won't you let them see my father?" the fairy asked the guards.

"They have brought the *liosta dubh*."

The fairy leader turned to Mr. Hamstead, who held Puck's bundled form in his arms. He pulled back the blanket to reveal the boy's fevered face. The leader blanched.

"Brother," he whispered.

"You're his brother?" Sabrina said. "But you're so . . . clean." Puck was usually covered in food and whatever he found in the forest to roll around in. She immediately wondered if Puck was adopted.

The fairy gingerly took Puck into his own arms, as if he weighed only as much as a baby.

"He's wounded, badly," Granny Relda said. "We can't help him, and we hoped your people might know what to do."

"Follow me," the boy fairy said as his wings vanished.

"But Mustardseed," one of the fairies protested. "Your father—"

Mustardseed turned to his friend with a hard stare. "My father will not hear of this, will he?"

The fairy's eyes were now alight with fear. "Of . . . of course not," he stammered.

Mustardseed strode through the double doors, taking Puck

with him. His friends followed, as did Sabrina and the others. He led them down a long, narrow hallway lined with oak doors and red wallpaper. It was lit with chandeliers and featured portraits of fairies in regal poses. At the far end was a pair of doors marked EMPLOYEES ONLY. The fairy shouldered them open and gestured for everyone to follow.

Sabrina found herself in a large, elegant library with hardwood floors. A roaring fireplace crackled on one side and a large oak desk sat on the other. A few high-backed chairs were scattered about. In one of them sat a woman wearing a dress that seemed to be made out of light. It engulfed her in a pale blue that made her glow like a distant star. Sabrina guessed she was in her late thirties. She had long brown hair and the same shocking blue eyes as Mustardseed. Her skin was pale, almost like milk. A pretty young girl around Sabrina's age stood behind the woman, gently combing her hair with a golden brush. When the group entered, the woman's eyebrows arched upward in suspicion.

"Mustardseed, if you are looking for your father, he is not here," the woman said.

"I will count it among my blessings," the boy said as he set Puck on a velvet sofa. "The crown prince has returned."

The woman and the young girl gasped in unison, rose to their feet, and rushed to Puck's side. They knelt down and brushed his matted hair off his sweaty face.

"Son!" the woman cried.

Sabrina was stunned. She'd assumed that Puck had a mother, but she hadn't given much thought to what she might look like. She'd sort of expected her to be old and broken, physically and mentally exhausted by Puck's pranks and immaturity, but this woman was young and healthy and seemed to be perfectly sane.

"Moth, find Cobweb—quickly!" the woman said to the girl. "Tell him to bring his medicines."

"But—"

"Go!" the woman shouted. Moth cringed and raced from the room as the woman turned her attention back to Mustardseed. "Where did you find your brother?"

"They brought him," he said, gesturing to the Grimms.

"What happened to him?" Puck's mother studied the group for the first time, her face full of suspicion.

"He was fighting a Jabberwocky, and it ripped off his wings," Sabrina explained, feeling a lump of guilt lodge in her throat. Puck had been trying to protect her when he was hurt.

The woman eyed her coldly. "And where would my son encounter a Jabberwocky?"

"Ferryport Landing," Daphne replied. "He lives there . . . with us."

"So that's where he went," Mustardseed said.

"Your Majesty, Queen Titania. It is quite an honor to meet

you. My name is Relda Grimm. I've been looking after Puck for some time now. These are my—"

"Grimm? More troublemakers?" the woman bellowed.

Sabrina sighed. Everywhere the family went, they got an angry reception from Everafters. Was this just old hatred of Wilhelm and Jacob . . . or had her father, Henry, been meddling in Everafter business in secret? Sabrina's heart sank. It seemed the longer they were in New York City, the more her old, normal life felt like a lie.

"You must know our father, Henry," Sabrina said, testing her theory.

"Your father? No! I'm talking about Veronica Grimm," Puck's mother said.

"Veronica?" the Grimms cried in unison.

"You know our mom?" Daphne said.

The woman fell back as if she'd been slapped. "Veronica Grimm has children?"

At that moment, Moth returned to the room. "Your Majesty, Cobweb is collecting his things and is on his way."

"Very good. Mustardseed, the presence of these people is no longer required. Escort them back to the park," Titania snapped.

"Whoa, whoa, whoa!" Mr. Hamstead said. "We're not just going to leave him here."

"He's part of our family, too," Daphne said.

"You can leave on your feet or in a box," the woman threatened.

Mr. Canis's eyes flashed blue. He stepped forward, fists clenched in rage. He started to open his mouth but was quickly interrupted by another angry voice.

"Well, well, well. I turn my back for one moment only to find my wife ready to plunge a knife into it!"

Sabrina spun around and found three large men entering the room. Two were the same goons Sabrina had seen tossing the naked man into the snow. Their leader was a stout, bearish man a bit older in appearance than Puck's mother. He had a big, thick face and thinning black hair. He was wearing a black suit, expensive shoes, and a gold watch. His wings fluttered furiously. All three of the men were carrying violin cases.

The leader charged at Titania, grabbed her roughly by the wrists, and shook her violently. "You've pushed me too far, Titania."

"Get your hands off me, Oberon!" the woman roared.

"Throw the traitor out of my kingdom!" Oberon ordered, pointing at Puck. His two huge cohorts moved toward the sick boy, but Mustardseed blocked their path.

"He's hurt," Mustardseed said.

Oberon turned his anger on his son. "Would you like to join your brother in banishment?"

Mustardseed shook his head, but he didn't move. "Your son needs your help."

"He's no son of mine," the king snarled, standing over Puck's weak body with clenched fists. "He turned his back on thousands of years of tradition. Banishment was a mercy. In the old lands, the King of Faerie could have had his head on a pike for such disobedience."

"What's a pike?" Daphne whispered to her sister.

"A long, pointy stick," Sabrina replied quietly.

Daphne cringed.

"You and your traditions are tearing this family apart. The old lands are dead and gone, Oberon," Titania said.

"Bah!" he scoffed. "Not for long!"

Just then, a tall, thin man with long black hair entered the room. His eyes were sunken and purple. He wore a leather suit that seemed to be made out of silk and spider webs. He carried a black case in one frail hand.

"You called for me," he said.

"Cobweb, I'm afraid you've wasted a trip. We won't be needing any medicine today," Oberon said, dismissing the fairy with a flick of his hand.

Sabrina was stunned. Would Oberon really let Puck die?

"No! Wait!" Titania cried. She pulled her husband aside, and her voice suddenly softened. "Let Cobweb heal Puck, and I will give you a present."

"What could you give me that I would ever want, Titania?"

"Power, Oberon," Titania said. "I can give you power over the entire Everafter community."

"I already control them," the fairy leader said with a laugh. His goons giggled with him.

"You don't have their respect. You don't have their admiration. They obey you begrudgingly, mostly due to tradition, but they are growing tired of waiting for your promised kingdom. How much longer do you have before they turn against you? I can give you something to capture what you've always wanted— their support."

"And what would that be, wife?" Oberon asked.

Titania gestured to Sabrina and Daphne. "The daughters of Veronica Grimm."

"Huh?" Sabrina said. "What are you talking about?"

Oberon laughed. "Another one of your lies."

Titania crossed the room and grabbed Daphne roughly by the wrist. "Tell the king who your mother is, human."

"Veronica Grimm," Daphne said, yanking her hand away.

"I think you've got the wrong Veronica Grimm," Sabrina said. "She wasn't involved in any Everafter business."

Oberon's eyes flashed so brightly Sabrina had to look away. He turned to Cobweb. "Heal the boy!" he commanded. "But when he is well he can go back to whatever rock he has been living under for the last ten years."

Mustardseed and Moth looked saddened by Oberon's declaration, but Titania nodded without argument.

Oberon spoke to the fairy in the tracksuit. "Bobby, I need the Wizard."

Bobby nodded, reached into his violin case, and took out a long, thin stick with a big silver star on the end. He waved it in circles above his head, and with a flick of his wrist a man suddenly appeared from nowhere. He was short and paunchy, with thinning hair and a big, bulbous nose. He wore gray trousers, a white shirt, and an emerald green apron covered in oil and dirt. He seemed completely bewildered, his eyes darting around the room in panic. Then he frowned.

"Blast it! How many times have I asked you not to do that, Your Majesty?" the man complained in a thick Southern accent. "I was in a staff meeting. An entire group of trainee elves and Santa Clauses just saw me disappear into thin air. They're probably falling over themselves in fear. You might think that forgetful dust grows on trees, but it's very expensive and harder and harder to get!"

"Wizard, your inconvenience means nothing to me. I need your particular talents," Oberon said. "Tonight we're having a celebration, and I want to see every Everafter in town. Tell them I have . . . a special surprise for them. Attendance is mandatory."

"A party? Tonight? Oh, no. That can't be done," the Wizard

argued. "That requires weeks of planning. Details have to be discussed, and then there's the signal. I can't just turn it on and off whenever you like."

The fairy with the bulldog face grabbed the Wizard by the shirt collar and lifted him up. "You're the Wizard. Nothing is impossible."

"Get your hands off me, you oversized fruit fly!" the little man cried.

Oberon stepped close to the man. "Wizard, you're the guy who makes miracles. Make one for me tonight."

The Wizard frowned but nodded. "I'll do my best."

"That's what I like to hear! Fat Tony, let him down."

The fairy did as he was told.

"I will need a little privacy with the prince," Cobweb said as he opened his case. He removed several vials containing liquids and powders, a few empty glass jars, and a mortar and pestle.

"Everyone out," Titania demanded as she exited the room. Moth and Mustardseed followed close behind, leaving the Grimms and their friends alone with the Wizard, Oberon, and his oversized henchmen.

The king turned to his men and gestured at Sabrina and her family. "Keep them somewhere safe. We don't want the community's Christmas present damaged before they get to open it, right?"

"Will do, boss," Bobby and Fat Tony said at the same time.

They turned to the family and cracked their knuckles threateningly.

"Keep your hands to yourself, or you'll lose them," Canis snarled.

Granny took his arm. "It's all right, old friend, we'll go with them."

Bobby and Fat Tony led the family out into the hallway. Sabrina felt Daphne slip her hand into her own and squeeze tight.

"Don't worry," Sabrina whispered to the little girl, wishing she could take her own advice. She had no idea what Oberon's henchmen had in store for them. They had hands as big as pumpkins and acted as if they had seen too many mobster movies.

"The boss wants you to wait in here," Bobby said when he stopped at one of the many doors in the hallway. He roughly shoved everyone inside before slamming the door closed. The room was full of boxes and extra tables and chairs that matched the furnishings in the main room.

"Wait a minute!" Sabrina cried. "You can't lock us up."

"We can't?" Fat Tony said from the other side of the door.

"I thought we just did." Bobby laughed.

"You're not very nice," Daphne shouted. "What kind of Everafters are you?"

"We're fairy godfathers," Fat Tony said.

"I've never heard of fairy godfathers."

"And that's just how we like it," Bobby replied. "Now, you sit in there and keep your mouths shut, and no one will get hurt."

Sabrina heard the lock turn. The men's muffled conversation faded as they walked down the hall.

"Veronica was a real looker," Bobby said.

"She had great gams, too," Fat Tony added.

"What does *gams* mean?" Daphne asked when the men were out of earshot.

"They liked her legs," Sabrina replied.

"Relda, I could easily knock this door down," Mr. Canis said. "Overpowering those two fools would be child's play."

"You can count on my help," Hamstead said.

"And we may need you both," Granny said. "But Puck's health is what's important right now. I'd rather not cause a ruckus until I know he's well. I don't believe we are in any danger."

"Not in any danger?" Sabrina cried. "Oberon says he's giving us away to the Everafters. I think we should go get Puck and break out of here right now."

"Then the boy will certainly die," Canis said. "I believe your grandmother is right. We will play their game until Puck is back on his feet."

"I'm confused about one thing. Why does everyone seem to know Mom?" Daphne asked. "Wouldn't it be cool if she was a fairy-tale detective, too?"

"Don't be so gullible," Sabrina said.

"I'm not being gullible!" the little girl insisted. "What does *gullible* mean?"

"It means you believe everything you're told. Oberon and the others couldn't have known Mom. She wasn't part of the family business. Dad would never have been OK with it, either. He moved to Manhattan to get away from the craziness in Ferryport Landing. Remember, this is Puck's family! He's the Trickster King! I bet pulling pranks is a family tradition. I'm sure this is all some big joke."

"I'm not so sure," Granny said. "Your mother was a Grimm, after all. She may have been involved with this community."

"My mother is a Grimm by marriage," Sabrina said a little louder than she intended.

"I'm a Grimm by marriage, *liebling*," the old woman said. "And, the life I married into is pretty enticing."

"Actually, your mother seemed to love detective work. She and your father got into a number of adventures in the short time she lived in Ferryport Landing," Mr. Hamstead said.

"Adventures?" Mr. Canis grumbled. "More like near-death experiences. The only thing that slowed her down was when she found out she was pregnant with you."

"She was a natural. Veronica fit into the family very nicely," Granny Relda said with a smile. "She might not have had Grimm blood running through her veins, but she certainly had a healthy dose of the family spunk."

"Stop it! Stop it! Stop it!" Sabrina yelled. Nobody knew Veronica better than she did. Her mother was a normal, everyday, predictable person who enjoyed reading, museums, and spending time with her children. She was exactly what Sabrina wanted to be when she grew up. She turned to her grandmother. "This can't be true, and we should get out of here now!"

Granny shook her head. Sabrina wanted to argue more, but she knew it was pointless. When the old woman made up her mind there was no use trying to change it.

The family waited for over an hour in near silence. After some time, Bobby and Fat Tony brought them a dinner of antipasti, salad, stuffed shells, and lemon chicken. It smelled delicious, and Sabrina was starving. Mr. Canis sniffed it and assured everyone that there was nothing unusual about the food, but she still wouldn't eat.

Some time later, the door opened and the man Oberon called the Wizard entered. He looked frazzled, as if he had spent the past hour pulling out what little hair he had left on his head.

"I'm real sorry about the inconvenience, folks," he said, but he couldn't get out another word before Mr. Canis sprang, knocking him to the ground. His fangs hovered dangerously close to the Wizard's neck.

"We have questions," Canis growled. "And we're tired of waiting for answers. How is the boy?"

"I don't know anything! Cobweb has been locked in that room with him for hours," the Wizard cried. "All I know is what the king told me. You're supposed to come with me. The party is about to start."

Mr. Canis turned to Granny Relda, who nodded. "Let him up."

The Wizard brushed himself off and checked his neck for puncture wounds, then said, "Listen, I'm just the messenger."

"And who exactly are you?" Hamstead asked.

"My dearly departed mother named me Oscar Zoroaster Phadrig Isaac Norman Henkle Emmannuel Ambroise Diggs." He reached into his pocket, took out a silver remote, pushed a button, and waited as a business card spit out of a slot in the front. He handed it to Granny Relda.

"*The* Oscar Zoroaster Phadrig Isaac Norman Henkle Emmannuel Ambroise Diggs?" she said.

"The one and only," the man said, then winked.

"Are you an Everafter?" Daphne asked.

"Yes, ma'am. My friends call me Oz."

Daphne let out a deafening squeal. She jumped around in a crazy jig. When she was finished, she stood shaking and giggling, biting down on the palm of her hand. After a moment, she removed her hand, launched herself at the stunned man, and wrapped her arms around him before he could stop her.

"You're my favorite!" she cried.

"Favorite what?" Oz asked.

"Favorite everything!"

"Well, it's always nice to meet a fan," he replied, squirming to free himself.

"Don't be too flattered," Sabrina mumbled. "She does the same thing when the pizza delivery guy shows up at the door."

Granny pulled the little girl away with considerable effort.

"I assume you are from Ferryport Landing. We don't get to meet too many of our neighbors from the north. None, actually," Oz said, quickly turning to Sabrina. "And I know you. I haven't seen you in years. Your momma used to bring you by the store all the time. I remember once we put you on Santa's lap to get a picture, and you wet your pants. Santa was furious. Oh, Veronica was so embarrassed, but I found it very funny."

*Liar!* Sabrina thought, blushing. She was tired of the game the Everafters were playing with her. "My mother never worked in a store."

"Oh no, I work in a store—Macy's department store, actually. Your momma and I were great friends. She visited me there often." Oz turned to Daphne. "And you must be Daphne. I held you when you were no bigger than a snow pea. You both look so much like her. The both of you are going to be great beauties."

He turned to address the rest of the family. "Folks, I'm truly sorry for all the hubbub. I'm sure you have a million questions, and I promise they will all get answered, but right now everyone is waiting for you."

"Everyone?" Sabrina asked.

He nodded, then led the family down the hallway and back into the restaurant. Every seat was taken by pirates, dwarfs, goblins, talking animals, even a human-size bug wearing glasses. All eyes were on a sultry, blond singer whose act brought catcalls and laughter from the audience. She wore a shimmering sequined dress and long, white gloves, and she prowled around the room flirting with the patrons while she purred through a song.

"Wow," Hamstead said. He seemed dumbstruck by the dazzling singer. "She's the most beautiful woman I have ever seen."

"And she's off limits, if you know what's good for you," Oz said. "Her name is Bess, and she's Fat Tony's girlfriend. He's the jealous type, if you catch my meaning."

Just then, Oberon and Titania entered the room, followed by Mustardseed, Cobweb, Moth, and more fairies. Their arrival was met by a chorus of boos and jeers from the crowd that forced the singer and the piano player to stop their lively performance.

"You've made us wait, Oberon!" an ogre shouted from his seat. "I've shared the same air with a Houyhnhnm for too long!"

A horse at the back of the room booed and stomped its hooves.

"Why have you brought us here?" a tiny porcelain doll cried from her seat. "I came all the way from Harlem. Do you know what the A train is like this time of day?"

"Friends, thank you so much for coming. I assure you it is going to be worth the inconvenience," Oberon said as he moved through the crowd.

The group exploded with anger. Many rose to their feet, shouting angry words about dirty fairy tricks and not being fooled again. Oberon seemed unconcerned, smiling into the angry crowd.

"Now, be nice or I won't give you your present," he said.

"What present?" an orangutan wearing a crown demanded.

Oberon rushed over to Sabrina and Daphne, grabbed each roughly by the arm, and dragged them onto the stage at the back of the room.

"What's the big idea?" Sabrina said, trying to pull away from his powerful grip.

Oberon ignored her and turned to the crowd. "Christmas comes to the kingdom."

"What is this nonsense?" asked a knight wearing a suit of green armor.

"Yahoo no want present from fairy," yelled an incredibly hairy man.

"Is that so? You don't want the children of Veronica Grimm?" Oberon cried.

The crowd instantly hushed. They sat motionless, watchful and suspicious.

*I knew it,* Sabrina thought. *They hate us here just like they do back in Ferryport Landing. They're going to kill us.*

# 3

SABRINA TOOK A DEEP BREATH AND BRACED herself for an attack. She had to be smart if she was going to get her family and friends out of the restaurant safely. She ran through the countless escapes she had made during her time in the foster care system. Finally, the answer popped into her head.

"Daphne, do you remember Mr. Drisko?" she asked.

Daphne nodded, then smiled.

Mr. Drisko was one of their more troubled foster parents; he made the girls share a bedroom with fifteen hyperactive ferrets. Sabrina once saw a documentary on television about ferrets. The narrator described them as furry, adorable, and playful, and suggested they made excellent house pets. The narrator would have changed his mind if he had met Drisko's ferrets. Sure, they were cute, but they were also evil. They bit Sabrina and Daphne every chance they got. They ate Sabrina's shoes and often relieved themselves on Daphne's pillow. Drisko said the ferrets were the loves of his life, and he doted on them like furry little babies. Unfortunately, Drisko's bad back and bunion-covered feet kept him from taking care of their most basic needs—feeding and bathing. It quickly became clear the girls were not taken in out of Drisko's sense of charity, but because he needed a staff to clean up the mess the ferrets made. Things went as well as could be expected until he insisted the girls give each one of the rotten little creatures a pedicure. When they refused, he tried to spank them. But, he never laid a hand on them. He never got a chance.

"On three," Sabrina said.

Daphne nodded.

"One! Two! Three!"

Together the girls stomped down hard on the tops of Oberon's toes. The fairy king yelped in pain and bent over to rub his feet. That was when the girls jumped on top of him and knocked him to the floor. They followed the tackle with a technique that never failed—relentless kicking. By the time Granny Relda reached them, Oberon was cowering on the stage in a ball.

"Are you OK, *lieblings*?" the old woman asked.

"We need to get out of here. This crowd is going to tear us apart!" Sabrina cried, taking her sister and grandmother by the hand. Fat Tony and Bobby were pushing through the crowd to

get to them, but if the family hurried, they could escape through the front door.

"Wait a minute! Do you hear that?" Daphne said, pausing at the edge of the stage. There was an odd noise coming from the crowd. It was laughter. The Everafters were falling out of their chairs, hooting and wheezing. Others applauded and rose to their feet. Soon they were all chanting the same word over and over again.

"Grimm! Grimm! Grimm!"

The Wizard rushed to Oberon's side and helped him to his feet. The fairy's face was red with rage. Oz whispered something in Oberon's ear, and the anger drained away.

"They're just like their mother!" Oberon shouted as he hobbled toward the Grimm family. The crowd roared with laughter again. "Prepare a feast. Tonight, we celebrate the daughters of Veronica Grimm! Tonight, her dream is reborn."

"What dream?" Sabrina asked, but no one answered. The Everafters circled the girls and lifted them onto their shoulders. They marched them around the supper club like they were heroes.

"What a glorious day!" Oberon shouted as the crowd set the two girls down in front of him and Oz, then rushed over to the bar where a round of celebratory drinks waited.

"You two have no idea what you've done," Oz said to the girls.

"You're right. I'm lost," Daphne said.

"Veronica Grimm was beloved by this community. When she

was here she worked with us to keep our kingdom alive. When she disappeared, many lost their commitment to our way of life. Now, you two can put us all back on the right path."

Granny Relda pushed through the crowd until she reached them.

"Your Majesty, we didn't come here to get caught up in local politics," she said to Oberon. "As soon as Puck is better, we need to be going. We have business at home that needs our attention."

"As you wish," Oberon said. His mouth was smiling, but his eyes were steely and serious. "You can go back to wherever you came from right after dinner. We'll eat, we'll drink, and then all the children have to do is back up every word I say. Afterward, I'll hand Puck over to you myself."

"What do you mean back up every word you say?" Hamstead asked suspiciously.

"This community needs to respect my rule. You must tell them Veronica supported my leadership."

Sabrina glanced at Oz. His face suddenly darkened. He looked as if he wanted to argue, but he held his tongue.

"Oberon, I'm afraid we can't do that," Granny Relda said.

Oberon scowled. "Why not!"

"Because we don't know if Veronica supported you or not," the old woman said. "We didn't even know she was involved with this community until ten minutes ago."

"And we have our doubts about that, too," Sabrina said. She still wasn't convinced all of this wasn't a mean-spirited practical joke.

Oberon rose to his full height. His eyes flashed with anger, and his mouth twisted into an ugly grimace. The crowd's chanting kept them from hearing his threat. "You do what I tell you to do."

"But—" Granny started.

Oberon interrupted. "My son's health does not have to improve."

"You are blackmailing us with Puck's well-being?" Granny cried.

"Whatever it takes to make you reconsider. I'll have Oz write up a speech for you." Oberon smiled.

He spun around and marched through the chanting crowd. Oz gave them a pained smile and followed his king.

"What are we going to do?" Hamstead asked.

Granny shook her head. "I don't know, Ernest. I just don't know."

The celebration dragged on and on. The Everafters danced and drank. Momma poured glass after glass as quickly as she could.

The girls were nearly as busy as the bartender. Everyone wanted to meet Veronica's daughters. The Everafters all had stories about their mother, too, how she inspired or helped them in some way. Each story broke Sabrina's heart a little bit more. Soon there was no denying that Veronica had had a life she kept secret from the rest of her family. Sabrina would never be able to think of her mom in the same way again.

And what to make of Oberon's demand? Sabrina didn't know much about these Everafters, but she knew she didn't like the king. Judging from the crowd's response to him earlier that evening, it seemed as if the Everafters shared her sentiment.

"He's a jerkazoid," Daphne said about him. The little girl was always coming up with her own words and sayings. *Jerkazoid*, as she explained it, was someone so jerky that they go beyond the levels of a normal jerk. "Kind of like a super jerk."

Oberon was a jerkazoid, but could he be telling the truth? Had Veronica actually supported him in his struggle for control? Sabrina couldn't be sure, because she had no idea who her mother was anymore. And even if Oberon was lying, how could the Grimms resist him? If he prevented Cobweb from helping Puck, the boy might die. What kind of a father would do such a thing?

While the girls were listening to praise from a woman who appeared to be wearing a dress made out of donkey skins, Oz pulled them away and ushered them to a quiet corner. He looked even more nervous and fidgety than when they had first met him. Without explanation, he tapped feverishly at the buttons on his silver remote. The device let out a few loud squeals and honks.

"Girls, your mother was one of the best friends I ever had, and it pains me to think that tonight Oberon will finally snuff out her legacy," Oz said. "Veronica would never tell the community she supported Oberon's rule. Most of the work she did on behalf of our people was because the king made their lives impossible. Plus, she was far too much of a diplomat to take sides, at least publicly. Privately, well, she and I spent many evenings talking about how great this community could be if he wasn't leading it."

"What do you want us to do about it?" Sabrina asked. "You heard his threat. He'll stop Cobweb from helping Puck."

Oz peered around the room again.

"Don't worry about the prince. Cobweb assures me Puck is out of the woods. Do what your mother would have done. Tell the crowd the truth. She thought Oberon was a fool. It will destroy the last shreds of support he has left."

"I don't think he and his goons are going to like it very much," Sabrina worried.

"Yes, it will be quite a kerfuffle, but I won't let anything happen to you. I have a few tricks up my sleeve, you know. I'll cause a diversion and smuggle all of you to safety, Puck included."

"Sounds good to me," Daphne said, rubbing her hands together eagerly. The little girl was fearless.

"Veronica would be proud of you," Oz said. He gave the girls a smile and slipped back into the crowd.

Soon, the Everafters were pulling tables and chairs together, making one long banquet table and covering it with food, candles, and malted beverages. Puck's brother, Mustardseed, appeared. He escorted the girls to seats at the head of the table. When they sat down, bowls of pasta with red sauce and plates of steaming meat were placed in front of them.

"Is this all-you-can-eat?" Daphne asked. "I'm starving!"

Mustardseed smiled and nodded. Canis, Granny Relda, and Hamstead found seats near the girls.

The beautiful singer took a seat next to Mr. Hamstead and introduced herself as Bess. Hamstead stammered his name, seemingly hypnotized by her beauty. To her left was her boyfriend, Fat Tony, who was already eating. He didn't even lift his head to acknowledge Bess's arrival but kept shoveling huge forkfuls of noodles into his mouth. She gave Hamstead an embarrassed smile, and his already pink face flushed bright red. He turned away, completely flustered.

"What's wrong with you?" Sabrina whispered in his ear. "Are you sick?"

"She's so pretty," Hamstead squeaked, nodding in Bess's direction. "What's she doing now?"

"She's looking at you and smiling," Daphne whispered. "She thinks you're foxy."

Hamstead's pig snout sprang onto his face, and he quickly covered it with his hand.

"Get a hold of yourself, Hamstead," he scolded himself.

Titania swept into the room, and Mustardseed helped her into her chair at the far end of the table. He took a seat next to her and patted her hand. It did little to erase the angry scowl on her face, which was directed right at the Grimms.

During the festivities, Oz had been called away, but now he returned from one of the back rooms. He approached Sabrina and leaned over to whisper in her ear. "Everything is all set."

"What's the diversion?" Sabrina whispered back, but before he could answer a chicken hopped into a nearby chair and flapped its wings furiously.

"Where's Oberon?" it cackled as it went to work on a plate of fat purple worms.

"Patience, Billina," Oz replied. "He's on his way."

Just as the Wizard leaned down to whisper to Sabrina again, there was a loud scream. The doors leading from the back hallway burst open, and Moth rushed into the room. Her face was twisted and red from crying, and her beautiful hair was flying in every direction.

"It's Oberon! It's the king!" she cried. She fell to her knees in despair and beat the floor with her fists.

Titania stood up so quickly she knocked over her chair.

"What is it, girl?"

"I found him in his office. He's been poisoned. He's . . . dead!"

The crowd let out a collective gasp.

Titania and Mustardseed rushed out of the room. The dinner guests jumped to their feet, knocking chairs and plates over in their excitement.

"Is this the diversion you were talking about?" Sabrina asked Oz.

The Wizard looked dumbstruck. "No! I have no idea what is going on!"

Granny Relda grabbed the girls, and with Canis and Hamstead in tow, they quickly found their way to the back hall. Together, they pushed through the crowd of Everafters to Oberon's office door. The sight inside made the blood freeze in Sabrina's veins. The king was lying on the floor next to his desk, a shiny gold cup clutched in his hand. His face was contorted in agony, as if the last moments of his life had been excruciating torture.

Titania threw herself on top of her husband and wailed with despair. Mustardseed tried to help his mother up, but she fought him off, and he backed away to let her grieve.

"Who killed my husband?" Titania cried. Sabrina was too distracted to listen. Oberon's chest was decorated with a horrible symbol. In bright red paint was a handprint. It was the mark of the Scarlet Hand.

# 4

SABRINA HAD NEVER SEEN ANGER IN A PERSON'S face like she saw in Titania's. The queen's rage seemed to pour out through her eyes and spill into the crowd like acid.

Everafters fell backward just to avoid her gaze.

"One of you killed my husband!" Titania shouted as she scanned the crowd. "Who is responsible? Who has blood on his hands? Will no one come forward?" The queen's body underwent a terrifying metamorphosis. Her already pale complexion turned bone white. Tar black veins curled in all directions just underneath her skin, weaving along her arms, legs, and head. Her hands grew to three times their normal size, and long, jagged nails, several feet in length, shot out of the fingertips. Her hair blazed with actual flames, and long, blue cables of electric energy crackled and popped in the air in front of her eyes. Her wings sprang out of her back and flapped so hard they seemed to shake the room. "Then I'll avenge my beloved by killing you all!"

She rose above the crowd, opened her mouth, and sprayed the room with a fiery blast. Everything it touched was quickly engulfed in flames and reduced to ash.

The crowd shrieked and stampeded toward the door, trampling one another in their effort to get to safety. Mr. Canis snatched the girls up before they could be crushed and tucked them under his arms like footballs.

"We have to get out of here," Granny Relda shouted as she was shoved aside by Fat Tony and Bobby.

"Wait! Bess!" Hamstead cried, then turned and ran head first into the rushing mob.

"Ernest, are you crazy?" Granny Relda called after him.

Sabrina was sure Hamstead would be stomped to death, but the portly man was fast on his feet. He darted through the crowd until he found the blond songstress cowering before Titania's murderous gaze. Fat Tony had left her behind.

"Back off, lady!" Hamstead cried as he grabbed a heavy chair and used it to fend off Titania. The queen spit fire at him, and the chair lit up like a match. If Hamstead was afraid, he didn't show it. He tossed the charred furniture at the queen and then helped Bess to her feet. Together they raced out of the room along with Canis and the Grimms.

When the group reached the main room, Daphne dragged everyone to a stop.

"We need to keep moving," Mr. Canis cried.

"We can't leave without Puck!" Daphne insisted.

He snarled but relented. "Hamstead, you and your friend should take Relda and the girls to safety. I'll join you once I find the boy."

"I'm coming with you," Sabrina said.

Canis shook his head. "It's too dangerous."

"It's my fault Puck is hurt. He's my responsibility," Sabrina said.

"Stay close," he said in surrender, and the two of them shoved back through the crowd. She followed at his heels, craning her neck in hopes of spotting Cobweb. Unfortunately, he was nowhere in sight. She guessed that he and Puck were still in one of the rooms that lined the back hall.

"Maybe Puck's in there," Sabrina shouted to Canis over the chaos, pointing to the first closed door. She tried the knob, but it was locked tight. When Canis grabbed the knob, it crumbled in his powerful hand. He pushed the door open only to find a broom closet. Sabrina rushed to another door, also locked. Canis took care of it as well and found Moth pacing back and forth next to what looked like a giant, slimy eggplant. Its deep purple skin was webbed with green veins. When she noticed Sabrina and Canis, Moth leaped in front of the eggplant as if to protect it.

"Titania is attacking everyone," Mr. Canis said as he stepped inside, shutting the door tight behind them.

"She won't hurt me. I am a privileged member of her court. Now go away. I have duties to attend to, and you are wasting my time."

"We're not going anywhere without Puck. Where is the boy?" Mr. Canis demanded.

The fairy girl's eyes narrowed with suspicion. "If you must know, he's in this chrysalis while his wings heal," Moth explained as she pointed to the sticky, purple sac.

"That's Puck?" Sabrina said incredulously.

Just then, something heavy slammed against the door, nearly knocking it off its hinges.

"That's Titania," Moth said. "I hope you aren't foolish enough to be in this room when she gets through the door."

"How are we going to get out of here?" Sabrina cried.

Mr. Canis searched the room for other exits but found none. He turned to Sabrina, the worry on his face morphing into aggression. His body doubled in size as his face took on wolflike features, until he was somewhere between the old man she knew and the wolf she feared. He stomped over to the far wall and pounded it with an enormous hand. It exploded into dust, and a hole appeared in the center. He pummeled it again, and the hole grew until it was big enough to step through.

"Who are you, Everafter?" Moth cried.

"He's the Big Bad Wolf," Sabrina explained, hoping it would frighten her into cooperating with them.

"The murderer?" the fairy girl shrieked.

"Come," he growled.

"I'm not going anywhere with you!"

"That's fine with me. Stay here in your crazy kingdom." Sabrina raced to the chrysalis and snatched it in her arms. It was surprisingly light but had a horrible smell like moldy pickles. She wrinkled her nose in disgust and ran through the opening with Mr. Canis following close behind. Moments later, Moth came flying frantically after them, her pink wings keeping her aloft.

"Give me the prince. Now!"

Sabrina heard another thump followed by a crash and looked behind her. Titania had knocked the door off its hinges. She shot a stream of fire that chased them through Canis's makeshift doorway and out into the cold street.

Canis ran down the path until, suddenly, they were back in the park, standing next to Hans Christian Andersen's statue. The Golden Egg was gone. Sabrina hurried alongside Canis, holding Puck and doing her best not to fall in the slippery snow. She turned an ankle and almost lost her hold on the chrysalis. As Sabrina righted herself, Moth landed in front of her and snatched the slimy cocoon out of her hands.

"You have no right to touch His Majesty's healing vessel," she said indignantly.

"You're getting in the way!" Sabrina said as she scanned the area for a hiding place. She suspected Titania wasn't going to just let them kidnap her son. A moment later, her suspicions proved true.

Titania appeared out of thin air, flying overhead and preparing to attack.

"Murder my husband and steal my son?" she screamed. "I will not have it!"

"We did not kill Oberon!" Sabrina shouted. "And Puck is a part of our family as much as he is yours."

"Then I will be there to help him mourn your deaths," she threatened.

Mr. Canis grabbed one of the tall lamps that lined the park's path and pulled it out of its concrete mooring. There were several loud pops as the electrical wires inside snapped, but not half as loud as when Canis swung the lamp and hit the queen in the ribs. The crash sent her hurling onto the pavement with enough impact to create a crater. Canis stood over the hole, waiting for Titania to crawl out.

"Stay down, fairy," he growled.

Granny, Daphne, Hamstead, and his new friend Bess appeared nearby. Granny's face fell when she saw what had happened in her absence.

"You will hang from the tallest tree for attacking the queen!" Moth bellowed.

Sabrina scowled. If they survived this, she needed to remember to introduce Moth to her fist. Just then, she heard the flutter of wings and watched as Mustardseed and his fairy army appeared in the sky and landed next to his unconscious mother.

"You must leave," he said. "I will take my brother."

"Forget it," Sabrina said. "Puck stays with us."

"I'm not arguing with you, child," Mustardseed said angrily.

"Then don't. I'm not letting him near your mother," Sabrina said.

"I'm confused," Granny said to Sabrina. "You're talking as if Puck is with us."

"He is," Sabrina said, pointing at the cocoon Moth was holding.

"This is Puck?" Daphne asked, placing her hand on the cocoon's skin. A sticky trail of goo clung to her fingers when she pulled it off. "Oh yeah, this is Puck all right."

"As Puck's fiancée, it is my honor and duty to protect the prince during his healing," Moth said.

"Wait? Fiancée?" the Grimms cried in unison.

Mustardseed seemed to weigh his options, then turned to Sabrina. "You may take him."

"Your Majesty!" Moth cried.

Mustardseed raised a finger, silencing Moth.

"If you take Moth with you. And you must not take Puck from the city. If you try, I cannot protect you from my mother's wrath."

"Sorry, buddy. We're out of here now!" Sabrina cried.

"Do not leave the city!" Mustardseed roared.

Granny Relda nodded. "We'll stay. You have my word."

The fairy looked relieved. "I must tend to my mother," he said. He and the other fairies lifted Titania off the ground, then flew back toward the statue, disappearing in a blink through the invisible portal.

Granny ushered everyone out of the park and didn't stop until they were several blocks away.

"We should check into a hotel," Granny said. "It's freezing, and I don't think this weather can be good for Puck. Plus, it will keep us off the streets if the chaos in the kingdom spills out of its borders."

"A hotel? We should go back to the car and get out of here as soon as possible," Sabrina said, shivering. "We have Puck. There's no reason to stay."

"I agree with the girl," Hamstead said.

"I gave Mustardseed my word that we would stay in the city," Granny Relda said firmly. "Besides, we're in the midst of a mystery."

"Another good reason to leave!" Sabrina said.

"Oberon is dead. The Everafters will need our help catching the murderer," Daphne argued.

"Daphne's right," Granny said. "We all saw the mark on Oberon's chest. The Scarlet Hand is behind his murder."

Before Sabrina could protest further, Fat Tony buzzed up to the group and landed next to Bess.

"I'm glad you got out OK, Bess," he said.

"No thanks to you," she muttered, then sighed as she turned to Mr. Hamstead. She leaned in close and kissed him on the cheek.

"A kiss for my hero," she said. "What do they call you, cowboy?"

"Er . . . Ernest," Hamstead said, clearly dumbfounded by her affection. His face turned pink, and he could barely pronounce his own name.

"That's enough of that, Bess," Fat Tony grumbled. He snatched his girlfriend by the wrist and dragged her back down the path toward the statue. Hamstead looked on wistfully.

Granny raised her hand, and a taxi pulled over. "We need to find a hotel with a parking lot," she said to the driver.

He shook his head and told them to leave their car where it was. "Parking is insane, lady," he explained, then told her he'd take them to the Fitzpatrick Manhattan Hotel, which he described as "pretty swanky."

Granny shrugged and helped Sabrina, Daphne, Moth, and Puck's cocoon into the back of the cab, then climbed into the front passenger seat. She rolled down the window to speak to Canis and Hamstead. "Can you two find it?"

Hamstead nodded. "We might be a little while. There's a couple things I think the two of us would like to see while we're here."

"Of course. I'll see you both at breakfast," Granny said, then urged them to be careful.

"What is stinking up my cab?" the driver cried, looking back at the purple sac in his rearview mirror.

"It's a school project," Sabrina lied. "Science fair stuff."

"What's the project? How quickly you can make a full-grown man lose his lunch?"

"Hey, it was no rose garden when we got into this taxi, you know," Sabrina said. "You ever clean these seats?"

The driver grumbled and pulled the car away from the curb.

Soon, the cab pulled up outside the Fitzpatrick Manhattan Hotel and the Grimms and Moth clambered out with the pungent cocoon. The hotel was a tall, distinguished building with an emerald green awning. A smiling doorman invited them into the toasty lobby where several tourists sat in front of a crackling fireplace, looking out the window at the falling snow.

"My goodness," one of the tourists cried as she pinched her nose. "I think the sewers are backing up."

Granny cringed and ushered the group to the front desk. She requested three rooms and asked that sets of keys be left for Mr. Hamstead and Mr. Canis. A bellhop looked at the group with an odd expression when he was told they had no luggage but said nothing. He escorted them to their room on the fourth floor. Inside they found two queen-sized beds, a lavish bathroom with a marble tub, and a pamphlet on the sights and sounds of the Big Apple.

"This is unacceptable," Moth said before they had even turned the lights on. "I am royalty and accustomed to finery. We need to find a more suitable room for the prince and me! One that is private!"

Sabrina rolled her eyes and ignored her.

"Hello, Mrs. Grimm," a voice said from across the room. Everyone in the group shrieked, even Moth, and fell over themselves in fright. There, sitting in a chair by the window, was Mustardseed. Oz was next to him. "I hope none of you were harmed this evening. I'm sure you can understand that my mother's actions were motivated by stress and heartbreak."

*Well, she nearly flame-broiled us back there!* Sabrina thought to herself. *Daphne would call her a jerkazoid.* Oz stepped forward. "As it turns out, Titania was the only one of us thinking clearly at the time. She ran everyone off to allow the killer a chance to escape."

"Escape?" Granny cried. "Why on earth would she want to do that?"

"To protect the new king," Mustardseed said. "Oberon's heir might have been the next target."

"What's an heir?" Daphne asked.

"Someone who inherits something from a relative," Sabrina explained, then turned back to Puck's brother.

"We are at a precarious point in our kingdom's history. There are many who would like to see it collapse entirely," Mustardseed said. "My mother and I will not allow that to happen."

"So you're saying your mother tried to barbecue everyone so she could protect you?" Daphne said.

Mustardseed shook his head. "You are confused. I am not the new king. That honor falls to my older brother, Puck."

"Puck is the new king?" Granny said, astonished.

"And your mother thinks we killed Oberon," Sabrina cried.

Oz nodded. "She initially suspected you because you're outsiders. Though I believe the prince has convinced her that you can be trusted. Besides, there is no way you could have been involved."

"Oberon was poisoned by an ancient concoction only a few learned fairies would know how to make," Mustardseed added. "It takes something very powerful to kill an Everafter, and something even stronger to kill one of my kind. The ingredients come from our fairy homeland. The recipe is a guarded secret. It couldn't have come from you and your family."

"Do you have any suspects?" Daphne asked.

"My father had many enemies."

"Unfortunately, whoever it was is now free on the streets of New York City," Oz said. "We know your reputation as detectives. The prince would like to hire you to help find the killer."

Sabrina tried to wrap her head around what was being asked of them. New York City was the home of nearly nine million people. It encompassed five different boroughs, linked by hundreds of miles of subway lines. Sure, Sabrina and Daphne knew parts of it as well as they knew their own faces, but most of the city was a complete mystery to them. It didn't make their task any easier that they knew next to nothing about the Everafters who lived there. This wasn't Ferryport Landing where everyone knew everyone. Where would the family even start looking for the murderer?

"This is not going to be easy," Granny said, obviously having similar thoughts.

"If you are even half as resourceful as Veronica Grimm, I have no worries at all," Mustardseed said.

"Folks, I'm afraid we've got one more favor to ask of you," Oz said. "Puck may be in danger. Keeping him safe is Titania's biggest priority. Do you think you can handle the responsibility?"

"Tell your mother that I love Puck like he is my own," Granny said. "I will keep him safe."

Mustardseed rose from his seat. "Moth, you will stay with the Grimms and assist them in any way they need. You will watch over your betrothed until he can safely return to the kingdom."

"For good?" Moth asked. "Is his banishment lifted?"

"It is a discussion for later," Mustardseed said. "But I will argue on his behalf. I want to be kept abreast of every development. I will be quite busy, so you can report your findings to Oz at the store where he works."

Moth smiled, then bowed. "You can put your faith in me."

"Oh, this is just getting better by the second," Sabrina said sarcastically.

Mustardseed bowed deeply to the family, then opened the window and leaped out into the night. Above the howl of the wind, Sabrina could hear the sound of mighty wings flapping. Oz closed the window tight.

"Any idea where we should start?" Daphne asked him.

The Wizard shook his head. "We don't exactly have an Ever-after phone book."

"Then how did you get them all to meet at the Golden Egg tonight?" Sabrina asked.

"I use the Empire State Building as a signal," Oz explained. "You may have seen them light it up for holidays. On Christmas, they use red, and on Saint Patrick's Day it's green. When we need to see everyone, we use bright purple."

"Perhaps we should try that," Granny said.

"I doubt anyone would show up after Titania's fit. I can tell you this much: I know the dwarfs live in the subway system, and I believe Sinbad lives somewhere down by the docks," Oz said.

"That's it? That's all you know?" Sabrina demanded.

"I'll ask around and let you know if I can point you in a direction," the little man said. He apologized, admitting he wasn't giving them much to go on, then said his good-byes.

"We're in the middle of a mystery!" Daphne clapped, nearly bouncing in anticipation. "Where do we start?"

"Let's make a list of our clues so far," Granny Relda replied.

"Sabrina, could you find us an ink pen? I bet there's one in the desk."

"No," Sabrina whispered. "I don't want anything to do with this. We should all just go home."

The room grew quiet. Daphne and Granny Relda stared at her as if she were some kind of math problem with no solution. Sabrina had rarely felt so alone. Couldn't Granny see that ever since she and Daphne had become fairy-tale detectives, they were in the path of death and destruction everywhere they went? Just yesterday they had survived the Jabberwocky by sheer luck, and now they were jumping back into another dangerous adventure. What if one of them got hurt again—or worse, killed? What if their luck finally ran out?

"Sabrina, we can't turn our backs on these people," Granny said. The old woman's face was filled with disappointment. She didn't understand. None of them understood, and worse, it was obvious they all thought Sabrina was selfish. The sting of tears filled her eyes, and she quickly ran into the bathroom, closing the door behind her. She sat on the side of the tub and wept.

After a few minutes, there was a knock on the door, then it slowly opened. Granny Relda entered, sat down next to Sabrina, and put her arm around the girl's shoulders. Sabrina tried to pull away, but Granny held her tight.

"Tell me," the old woman whispered.

"I don't want to do this."

"Sabrina, these people asked for our help. It won't hurt us to look around and ask some—"

"No . . . I'm not talking about this mystery. I don't want to be a Grimm."

Granny sat quietly for a long time, and Sabrina prepared herself for a lecture about responsibility and doing the right thing.

"You don't have to, Sabrina," Granny finally said.

Sabrina was stunned.

"You were deposited into this life against your will. I thought that after some time you would get used to being a Grimm and see what a rewarding life it can be. But I realize now that I'm forcing you to do it, and that isn't fair. You do have a choice, and I should have explained it. Many have walked away from our family business. If you've ever read any of Douglas Grimm's journals, he often wrote about how miserable he was; even your Opa Basil had his doubts. And, of course, your own father made a choice to pursue a different life. You can do the same if it is really what you want."

"Sure, and you'll be disappointed with me. You'll give me that look you give me when you're angry," Sabrina said.

"No, I won't. I will, however, miss sharing the time with you," Granny said. "I truly believe you are becoming an excellent detective, but you can retire if you want. Perhaps it is best if you stay at home from now on, anyway. Someone besides Elvis needs to keep an eye on your parents."

"So you're not mad?"

Granny Relda kissed her on the forehead. "No, I'm not mad."

"I'd still like to help find a way to wake Mom and Dad," Sabrina said.

"Of course," the old woman said. "You can decide to get involved any way you like."

Sabrina felt as if the sun had come out and was shining just for her. The gnawing pain in her belly from endless worrying subsided for the first time in weeks.

"I can't wait to tell Daphne we don't have to do this anymore."

Granny frowned. "No, Sabrina. You get to make your choice. She gets to make hers."

"She's only seven years old," Sabrina argued.

"And you're only eleven, but I'm trusting you to be mature enough to make this decision about your life," the old woman said. "Daphne can work on mysteries as long as she likes. That's only fair."

"But—"

Granny shook her head. "Now, we're in the middle of a case to which I have committed us all, and honestly I need your help. Can I count on you for one more mystery? After that, you're done."

Sabrina nodded. She hadn't expected her grandmother to understand her choice, let alone support it. She could walk away from the

Grimm family legacy. No more Everafters, monsters, or lunatics. Now all she had to do was convince Daphne to make the same decision.

When the two Grimms left the bathroom, they found Mr. Hamstead sitting in the chair. He explained that Mr. Canis wasn't feeling well and had already gone to bed.

"Ernest," Granny Relda said, "I'm afraid we're going to be staying awhile. Mustardseed has asked us to find his father's killer. I understand if you need to get back to Ferryport Landing."

"Go home?" Mr. Hamstead said.

"Yes. We're going to be traipsing all over the city, finding Everafters and interviewing them about Oberon. You don't need to be here. I'll tell Bess you said good-bye."

"You're going to talk to Bess?"

"Of course. She was there when Oberon was poisoned, after all."

"I'll stay," he said with a smile. He was clearly looking forward to seeing the beauty again. Something told Sabrina her grandmother had just manipulated Hamstead into helping with the case.

Daphne clapped her hands. "What's the plan?"

"The plan, Daphne, is to get some rest. Tomorrow we're going to track down a killer."

"Where are we going to start?" Sabrina asked as she looked out the window at the massive city nestled beneath a blanket of snow.

"I think we should start with the one person we know the best. I want to find out more about your mother. We'll start at your old apartment," Granny replied.

The plan for the morning was to split up. Hamstead would search the lower part of the city, and the Grimm family would handle the upper part. When they knocked on Mr. Canis's door, he told Granny Relda that he needed time to meditate. She agreed that he should rest for the day. Sabrina wondered if she'd noticed the new wolfish whiskers on the old man's chin.

The group finished breakfast in the hotel's restaurant and met in the lobby. They were surprised to find they had a visitor. Bess was sitting by the fireplace wearing a long winter coat and a silver backpack.

Hamstead's face lit up like the Rockefeller Center Christmas tree.

"Care for a little help?" Bess asked as she smiled at Hamstead.

"Of. . . of course," Hamstead stammered. "But won't this cause some waves with your boyfriend? I don't think he likes us much."

"It might, but I don't particularly care. I dumped the jerk this morning."

"We're happy to have the help," Granny said, shaking Bess's hand. "Why don't you team up with Ernest?"

"What do you say, cowboy?" she asked the portly sheriff. "Want a sidekick for the day?"

He nodded enthusiastically.

As the group stepped out onto the sidewalk, they found that two feet of snow had fallen in the night, turning the city into a winter wonderland. They split up, wishing each other luck. Hamstead and Bess went south, while Granny, the girls, and Moth searched for a cab to head north. After ten minutes without success, they caught a bus that took them uptown to the girls' old neighborhood on the Upper East Side. Unfortunately, where Moth went, Puck's smelly chrysalis went, too. No one wanted to sit next to the slimy thing, which leaked a funky, rotten-egg gas. Sabrina spent most of the ride avoiding the angry looks of the other passengers.

"Well, it appears your mother had a secret life," Granny Relda said as the bus headed up Madison Avenue. "Several of us have gotten into the family business through marriage. Myself, for example. I'm hoping she kept the family tradition of writing down what she experienced for future generations."

"You mean a journal? Do you think she kept one?" Daphne asked. Sabrina had a journal, too, though she rarely kept a record of what she had encountered. Writing it down made it more real. Daphne, on the other hand, was already working on her second volume.

"It's possible," Granny said. "If so, she hid it well. Your father was dead set on breaking ties with the Everafter community. If he had discovered his wife was solving cases behind his back, he would have been very angry. My theory is the book is still somewhere in your old apartment."

"How much longer am I to suffer inside this rolling tin can?" Moth groaned. "The constant jostling is upsetting the prince and my delicate constitution."

"What did she say?" Daphne asked her sister.

"She's complaining," Sabrina explained. "As usual."

After several stops and a lot more whining from Moth, they finally exited the bus at the corner of East Eighty-eighth Street and Madison Avenue. Then they headed east across several avenues until they reached York Avenue. This was a quiet little nook of the city filled with families, dogs, and older people. As Sabrina looked around, a wave of nostalgia flooded over her. There was the little deli that sold the roast-beef-and-gravy sandwiches her father used to sneak out to buy late at night. Down the street was Carl Schurz Park, where her family had spent many afternoons looking out over the East River or playing with puppies in the little dog run. Across the street was the luxury apartment high-rise their mother often dreamed they'd live in one day. Sabrina spotted Ottomanelli's Café with its amazing meatball pizza, the dry cleaner where the Cuban lady always gave her lollipops, and the magazine store owned by the guy who let his three cats sleep on stacks of the *New York Times*. Sabrina could even smell the world's best brownies from Glaser's Bake Shop a block away. Little had changed, except that the old skateboard store was now a manicure shop.

They walked along East Eighty-eighth Street, past a group of five-story brownstones, and quickly reached their old apartment building at number 448. There was a fresh coat of gray-blue paint on the once yellow facade, but aside from that, the place was exactly how she remembered it.

"We can't get in," Sabrina said as they climbed the freshly salted steps. "The police took our keys when they sent us to the orphanage."

"Sabrina, those old keys wouldn't work anyway," her grandmother said. "There's a new family living here, and I'm sure they've changed the locks."

Sabrina blinked back unexpected tears. She had never imagined that strangers might actually be living in their home.

"So someone else lives here?" Daphne whispered. Sabrina could hear her own dismay echoed in her sister's voice.

Granny nodded as she pushed the doorbell that rang in their old apartment.

"Hello, who is it?" a voice crackled from the speaker.

"Um, yes, so sorry to bother you, ma'am. My name is Relda Grimm. I'm here with my granddaughters, who used to live in your apartment—"

A buzzer sounded, and the door unlocked before the old woman could finish her sentence. Granny led them inside and down the hall to their old apartment. The Grimms were halfway there when an excited woman wearing huge red glasses threw open the door.

"I'm so thrilled to meet you," she said.

"I hope we aren't imposing," Granny Relda replied. "We were in the neighborhood."

"Nonsense, I've always wanted to meet the previous owners," the woman said, holding out her hand. "My name is Gloria Frank."

"I'm Relda Grimm. These are my granddaughters, Sabrina and Daphne . . . and Moth."

"Hello, peasant," Moth said, awkwardly hoisting Puck's chrysalis onto her shoulder.

Gloria looked confused but smiled. "Please, come in."

For Sabrina, stepping into the living room was a shock. Their once colorful home was now painted in drab shades of beige. The hardwood floors were freshly varnished, stealing all their old charm and personality, and many of the antique light fixtures had been replaced with modern lamps. All of the furniture Sabrina remembered was gone. Their big puffy couch was replaced with a sleek chocolate brown sofa that looked more like a work of art than something to sit on. Every photograph of her family was gone, and Daphne's finger paintings were no longer hanging on the refrigerator.

Just then, a teenage boy walked out of Sabrina's old bedroom. He was a lanky kid wearing a rugby shirt and carrying a tablet. His curly blond hair bounced at his ears, and he wore headphones that blasted music. When he saw the visitors, he took off the headphones and regarded the group curiously. "Mom? What is that awful smell?"

"His Majesty's healing vessel gives off an unusual scent, but it is not by any means awful," Moth said. "You should be honored to have found its aroma in your nose, you undeserving wretch."

"I'm so sorry," Granny said, stepping between Moth and everyone else. "My granddaughter is in a play, and she's been practicing her lines nonstop. Unfortunately, they're using some unusual props and she feels it's best to carry one with her."

"She's a method actress. How delightful! My son is an actor, too," Mrs. Frank said as she turned to her son. "What was the last play your school did? You were incredible in it. What was it called?"

"*A Midsummer Night's Dream.*"

"He played Puck. Do you girls know that play?"

"We're living it," Sabrina grumbled as the cocoon gave off a particularly noxious blast of funk.

"Phil, these girls used to live here," Mrs. Frank said, waving her hand in front of her nose. Then, seeming to realize that this might be rude, she pretended to smooth her hair instead.

"Wassup?" the boy said.

"You have my old bedroom," Sabrina said quietly.

Phil raised his eyes and nodded, then put his headphones back on and wandered out of the room.

"I'm sorry. Since we bought him that game, we can't get it away from him," his mother said. "Can I take your coats?"

"We can't stay," Granny said. "We just wanted to come by and see who lived here now."

"Oh, we really love the apartment. I hope you think we're taking good care of it," Mrs. Frank said.

Sabrina didn't answer. She kept glancing around the room, trying to find something she recognized. The whole experience was making her dizzy.

"Mrs. Frank, there is one other thing. We were wondering if you happened to find anything in the apartment when you moved in—say, for instance, a journal or a book of stories about fairy-tale characters?" Granny asked. "The girls' mother was a . . . a writer. She may have kept one, and we'd love to get our hands on it."

"Oh, we found a few things when we redid the kitchen and the closets," the woman said. She rushed out of the room and returned with an old shoebox. "My husband told me I was crazy to keep this stuff. He says I'm a pack rat, but they seemed personal and, well, it felt wrong to throw them out."

Sabrina took the box. Inside were a few yellowing love letters from their father, some scattered pictures of Sabrina and Daphne in the bathtub when they were little, and a wallet with pink roses sewn on the leather.

"No journal," Daphne said with a sigh.

"Oh, dear, it's not here," their grandmother said. "Do you think you might have overlooked it?" she asked Mrs. Frank.

Gloria shook her head. "We did a lot of work on this place

when we moved in. If there was a journal, we would have found it. I'm sorry."

"Well, we appreciate you hanging on to these things for us," Granny said. "We should probably be going."

"It was so nice to meet you," Mrs. Frank said.

Granny and the girls waited at the bus stop until the next bus came. They climbed inside and found seats in the back. Moth chattered on about how ignorant human beings were, but the Grimms were silent. Sabrina sat by the window, watching her neighborhood disappear.

Back at the hotel, the little group waited for the elevator. When the doors opened, they were startled to see Mr. Hamstead and Bess inside, locked in a passionate kiss. When the couple finally noticed everyone staring, Hamstead's face glowed pink and his snout popped out. He quickly put his hand over it, eyeing Bess nervously as if he didn't want her to see. Bess, on the other hand, was grinning from ear to ear, holding him in her arms like they were lost at sea and he was her life preserver.

"Oh, hello," Granny said as the couple stepped out of the elevator. "Is Mr. Canis awake?"

"Yes," Hamstead said. "He's in his room and wants to speak with you. I asked him if everything was OK and he nearly bit my head off, literally."

"We just stopped by for some hot cocoa," Bess said. "Wall

Street was a bust. Our community is terribly fractured. We live such separate, secret lives. We're going to try SoHo and Chinatown next. I've heard Gulliver lives in Tribeca, but I don't have an address." The blonde turned to Hamstead and gave him a big, over-the-top smooch on the cheek. "Sugar dumpling, I need to freshen up. Mind if I borrow your room key?"

"Not at all," Hamstead said. He dug into his pocket and handed it to her. A moment later, she was back inside the elevator and on her way upstairs.

"Mr. Hamstead, I do believe you are quite smitten with her," Granny said.

"What does *smitten* mean?" Daphne asked.

Sabrina turned to answer but noticed something unusual. The little girl was asking Granny Relda instead of her.

"It means he's got a huge crush on her," Granny said.

"Which is a huge problem," Mr. Hamstead said. "When she finds out who I am . . . what I am—"

"Ernest, she's an Everafter, too, obviously," Granny Relda said.

"An Everafter with a human form," Hamstead said. "I'm a pig. There's a big difference."

"But there are lots of mixed-Everafter couples. You're forgetting Little Miss Muffet and the spider."

"Miss Muffet is a crackpot," Hamstead said. "Bess is beautiful and funny and the most amazing woman I've ever met. She's not going to be interested in me when she discovers I'm just an unemployed pig from upstate."

Granny smiled. "I'm sure Bess likes you for who you are."

"If this pointless conversation is over," Moth complained, "I'd like to get His Majesty back to the room."

"Of course," Granny said. "I'm going to pop in on Mr. Canis. I'll meet you there soon."

The girls went up to their room and closed the door. Moth climbed onto one of the two queen-sized beds and propped the icky cocoon onto a pillow. "I need silence, humans," she announced.

Sabrina rolled her eyes and turned to her sister.

"Fine. We need to talk somewhere that doesn't smell like a sneaker soaking in moldy lemons, anyway." She gestured to the bathroom, and Daphne followed her inside.

"Daphne, Granny and I have talked and we've come to an understanding—"

"I know all about it," Daphne said stiffly.

"Then you know I'm not going to be involved in this detective stuff anymore. I don't want you to do it, either," she said, sitting on the side of the tub. The twinge of guilt rolled up her spine. Granny had asked her not to try to talk her sister out of solving mysteries, but the old woman didn't see it as clearly as Sabrina. The family business was far too dangerous for Daphne without her older sister around. "We should be trying to find out how to wake Mom and Dad up, anyway. Once they're back to normal, we can move back to Manhattan and be a family again. Doesn't that sound good?"

Daphne burst into tears. They streamed down her face and onto the shoebox Gloria Frank had given them. She still had it clutched in her hands.

"Why are you crying?" Sabrina asked, dismayed. "Don't you want to go back to how things used to be?"

"No!" Daphne yelled. "This is our destiny."

"You don't even know what the word *destiny* means." For the first time in Sabrina's life, she saw rage in her little sister's eyes. Before Sabrina knew what was happening, Daphne set down the shoebox, reached behind Sabrina, and turned on the water, soaking her sister.

"What was that for?" Sabrina sputtered. "I'm trying to protect us."

"No you're not! You're trying to control me. You haven't once asked what I want. You're a . . . jerkazoid, and I don't need you. I'll be a fairy-tale detective all by myself!" Daphne turned and stomped out of the room, slamming the bathroom door behind her.

Soaked to the bone, Sabrina climbed off the tub, took off her clothes, and put on one of the fancy white robes the hotel kept in the closet. She wrapped her hair in a towel and thought about what her sister had said. Daphne didn't get it. She was too young to understand how dangerous their lives were on any given day. Sabrina would have to find a way to make her understand.

The little girl had left the shoebox sitting on the toilet tank. Sabrina picked it up and opened the lid. The photos were the embarrassing bathtub shots that parents loved and kids hated, but they made Sabrina smile. They showed happier times. She flipped through the yellowing love letters, tied with a small red ribbon, and then opened the wallet. Inside were her mother's driver's license, some expired credit cards, a couple of pictures of her father, and a photo of Veronica sitting with her daughters on a bench. Sabrina's and Daphne's faces were painted with stars and rainbows. They were both smiling. That day was clear in her memory. Her mother had taken them to a fair held at the South Street Seaport—it was a good day.

How odd it was to hold something her mother had owned. The girls hadn't been able to keep a single item from their old lives; even their clothes were gone. Having these things was the answer to a prayer Sabrina had said a hundred times. She lifted the wallet to her nose and sniffed the worn leather deeply. She swore she could detect a faint hint of her mother's lilac perfume.

# 5

DAPHNE WAS NOT TALKING TO HER AND Moth was shooting her angry looks, so Sabrina turned back to the book about Puck's family her grandmother had given her: *A Midsummer Night's Dream*. It was a play, mostly about Oberon and Titania, but Puck was a big part of it. Mustardseed, Cobweb, and Moth were in it as well. Though the old-fashioned language was challenging to read, it didn't take a brain surgeon to realize Shakespeare's head was full of fairy nonsense. Maybe that was why he'd gotten Puck's relationship with his father wrong. In the play, Puck wasn't Oberon's son, just some annoying beastie that made mischief. Who knew, maybe Oberon had refused to admit to the writer the truth about his embarrassing son. The king certainly hadn't seemed to care about Puck when the family brought his son to him for help. One thing Shakespeare had gotten right: Oberon and Titania were selfish and weird.

When Granny finally returned to the room, Mr. Canis was with her. Except for a glimpse that morning, Sabrina hadn't seen him since the night before. She was shocked at his appearance. He had grown several inches in height and packed on twenty pounds of muscle. His shock of white hair was now streaked with brown, and he had the definite beginnings of a beard and mustache. Whenever Canis tapped into the Big Bad Wolf's power, he seemed to lose a little more of himself, but this was a dramatic transformation. She wondered what the family would do when there was no more of Mr. Canis to lose, but she said nothing. The topic seemed off limits, and Granny acted as if all was well. She was eager to get back on the case and urged the girls to hurry with their coats, hats, and mittens.

Most of the day was a waste of time. They scurried from one neighborhood to the next, hoping to stumble upon an Everafter. Bess gave them plenty of leads, but they all turned out to be dead ends. Still, Granny Relda was determined. She must have poked her head into every dark restaurant and creepy alley in Manhattan, questioning dozens of street people, who knew more neighborhood secrets than anyone. Many were homeless, and Granny Relda thanked them for their time and information with five-dollar bills, insisting they use the money to put something warm in their bellies. None of their tips turned into an actual lead. The closest the detectives got to a magical creature was a man riding a multicolored bicycle around Washington Square Park wearing a wedding dress. But he turned out to be human.

With Mr. Hamstead and Bess no doubt sharing a romantic meal somewhere, the rest of the investigators decided to stop for an early dinner at a small Chinese restaurant called the Happy Duck. As they went inside, Sabrina noticed eight roasted ducks hanging in the window. They didn't look very happy to her.

The restaurant was the kind of place where the menu was as big as a dictionary. The staff spoke little English and the tables were crowded together. The waiters eyed Puck's chrysalis and pinched their noses at its gassy belches. The group made their way to a table in the back near a huge aquarium filled with milky water and fat koi fish. Daphne ordered enough food for the whole table and several others. Sabrina welcomed the break from tramping through the snow, but dinner turned out to be anything but relaxing. Granny kept hurrying off to make phone calls. Mr. Canis sat silently with his eyes closed, breathing in and out in a slow pattern. Puck's icky vessel kept rubbing up against Sabrina, coating her in sticky goo, and Moth refused to eat, saying the food was a travesty unfit for pigs. The whole ordeal stressed Sabrina out more than the endless goose chase trying to find Everafters.

"Your Uncle Jacob says all is well," Granny said when she returned to the table.

"Has he found a way to wake up Mom and Dad?" Sabrina asked hopefully.

Granny shook her head. "He says he's trying every magical potion we have in the Hall of Wonders. Unfortunately, he's been forced to abandon our home for a couple of days."

"Why? What happened?"

"He made the mistake of giving Elvis a plate of sausage."

There was one major rule when it came to the family dog: no sausages! They did bad things to the two-hundred-pound Great Dane's belly—very bad, very smelly things. The last time Daphne gave him one they almost had to move.

"I miss Elvis," the little girl said. She leaned back in her chair and rubbed her protruding belly. "Look at me. I'm having a food baby. I'm going to name him Number Fifteen with Egg Roll."

Granny laughed. "*Liebling*, you've got food all down the front of your shirt. Let me take you into the bathroom and clean you up."

Daphne shrugged as if she didn't care, but Granny insisted.

"I believe I would like to wash my hands," Mr. Canis said abruptly, and he, too, got up from the table, leaving Sabrina and Moth all alone. Sabrina tried to ignore the fairy girl, but Moth's angry eyes were boring into her.

"Let's make something clear, human," Moth said. "If you attempt to interfere in my relationship with Puck you will regret it. He is my fiancé!"

"Listen, I don't want your fiancé. I'm eleven. I'm not even allowed to have a boyfriend, so when Puck finally crawls out of this icky pumpkin he's all yours."

"You do not love him?" Moth said.

"NO!" Sabrina said, a little too loudly. She looked around the room and felt every eye on her, including those of Mr. Canis, who was waiting in line for the bathroom. "I do not want anyone to confuse Puck when he finally reconsiders Oberon's choice," Moth said.

"What are you talking about? What is Oberon's choice?"

"Me. I am Oberon's choice. He selected me to be Puck's bride," Moth said.

"What do you mean he selected you?"

"It's called the father's privilege. Fairy fathers choose their sons' mates."

Sabrina laughed. "I wish I could have seen Puck's face when his dad made that announcement!"

Moth snarled, and Sabrina realized the girl took the subject very seriously.

"So then what happened?" Sabrina asked.

"The prince was confused . . ."

"You mean he dumped you," Sabrina said.

"He made a mistake, and, unfortunately, his father punished him for it. Puck was banished from the kingdom. That was more than ten years ago, and not a word has been heard from him since . . . until yesterday," Moth said.

"He's been trapped in Ferryport Landing. It's like a big roach motel. You can check in, but you can't check out," Sabrina said.

"Besides, from what I know of him you're better off without the Trickster King. He's kind of a pain in the neck."

"How dare you!" Moth cried as she rose to her feet. "King Puck is a great fairy."

"Calm down," Sabrina said. "I'm not saying he doesn't have some good qualities."

Moth sat back down, but her face was still angry.

"What makes you think it's going to be different this time, Moth?" Sabrina continued. "Puck left town to avoid marrying you once. Why don't you think he'll do it again?"

Moth snarled but said nothing.

"Well, I wish you luck," Sabrina said sarcastically. "The Trickster King is a real catch."

The two girls sat in silence. Sabrina couldn't help but notice how pretty Moth was, how poised and confident she seemed. She tucked her own hair behind her ears and started to tame some loose strands hanging in her eyes.

"Who wants some lychee ice cream?" Daphne cried, when she and the others returned to the table.

"You're still hungry?" Mr. Canis asked.

"I'm still awake, aren't I?"

While everyone looked over the dessert menu, Sabrina reached for her mother's wallet. She'd tucked it into her coat pocket, liking the way it felt when she touched its cool leather. She flipped it open to sneak a peek at her mom's pictures and credit cards. She uncovered a small flap hidden behind a picture of her father. Behind it was a business card. It was dark blue and covered in little moons and stars. It had an inscription in silver ink:

*Scrooge's Financial and Spiritual Advice*
*Affordable Rates!*
*18 West 18th Street*
*Voted Best Psychic by* Time Out New York *magazine*

Sabrina flipped the card over and found handwriting on the other side.

*Veronica, stop by anytime. I owe you one!*
*E. Scrooge*

"What's that you've found?" Granny Relda asked.

"Just some old business card in Mom's wallet," Sabrina said, handing it over. "I think it's for a psychic or something."

Granny read the inscription and grinned.

"Sabrina, for someone who doesn't want to be a detective, you're very good at finding clues!"

Sabrina was dumbfounded. "Clues? It's just a card for some scam artist. There are psychics all over the city."

"Whether he's a real psychic is beside the point. He's a real Everafter, and we've got his address."

Daphne took the card and read the inscription. "What makes you think he's an Everafter?"

"Look at the name on the card—E. Scrooge!"

"Yeah, so?" Sabrina said.

"E. Scrooge . . . as in Ebenezer Scrooge," Granny said.

"The cranky rich guy from *A Christmas Carol*?" Daphne asked.

"The one who was visited by ghosts?" Sabrina asked.

"The one and only," Granny said.

"I'm going to freak out!" Daphne bit down hard on her palm.

Eighteenth Street was a pothole-riddled road in Chelsea, a neighborhood in lower Manhattan. As the group made their way to Scrooge's shop, they passed an art supply store, a vintage record outlet, a children's bookstore, and several places where a person could buy mannequins and sewing machine parts. Scrooge's Financial and Spiritual Advice was in the middle of the block. In the grimy window was an enormous green neon sign with an eye that blinked every few seconds below the words SPIRITS AND SAVINGS BONDS.

Sabrina studied the sign for a moment, running through everything she knew about Scrooge. Charles Dickens had documented the story: A greedy businessman was visited by the Ghosts of

Christmas Past, Present, and Future. Sabrina had seen the musical on Broadway when she was little and remembered Scrooge clearly as greedy and mean.

His waiting room was crowded with a mob of weirdos. They all wore themed costumes from every holiday imaginable—patriotic uniforms with sparklers, bright emerald suits covered in shamrocks, turkey costumes, cupid outfits—there was even a guy wearing a big paper top hat and a pair of glasses that read HAPPY NEW YEAR!

The family approached an empty desk at the far end of the room. A little sign on top read TIM CRATCHIT. Next to it was a silver bell with another sign that read RING BELL FOR SERVICE. Granny tapped it, sending a chiming sound into the air.

"I'll be right out!" a voice shouted from behind a closed door near the desk. The voice was followed by a mechanical sound, like an engine, and another noise, like something heavy crashing into a stack of fine china. Moments later, a kid with a round face and freckles appeared in the doorway on a motorized chair. He seemed to have no control over the machine and repeatedly slammed it into the doorframe. After several failed attempts to roll forward, he finally got the chair through the narrow doorway. Unfortunately, his problems didn't stop there. Once he entered the room, he slammed into the desk and sent it toppling on its side.

"Blast it!" the kid shouted in a thick English accent. He tried to pull the desk upright and nearly tipped himself onto the floor in the process. Exhausted just from watching him, Sabrina stepped in and righted the desk. Once the boy was comfortably situated, the waiting room crowd rushed forward, jostling the Grimms to the back of the line. Everyone argued at once.

"I have to be somewhere in fifteen minutes," said the man wearing New Year's glasses. He took a small plastic horn out of his pocket and gave it an angry toot.

"Well, I was here first," a giant complained as he pushed himself to the front. He was covered in leaves and pinecones and smelled like a forest.

Tim Cratchit whistled loudly, and the crowd grew silent. "Are any of you paying customers?"

"C'mon, Tim!" an enormous man in a bunny suit said. "We've been waiting all day."

"And you'll wait all night!" Tim cried. "You buggers show up anytime you please. Mr. Scrooge is a busy man and hasn't the time to waste on a bunch of penniless layabouts."

"Uh, we can pay," Granny said.

Tim's eyes searched for her in the crowd, and then he smiled. "Are you alive?"

Sabrina and Daphne eyed each other.

"Last time we checked," Sabrina said.

"Well, I can't just take your word for it," Tim said as he accidentally pushed a button that sent the chair slamming into the desk again. "We're very busy here, and paying, living customers have priority, but you've got to prove both to me."

His words caused the crowd to erupt in protest.

"You want proof that we're alive?" Mr. Canis asked as he and the others approached the desk. "How do we do that?"

The boy reached over to Sabrina and Daphne and gave them both painful pinches on the arm. They yelped angrily, and Daphne kicked the boy's chair.

"OK, I'm satisfied. Now, are you here for the boss's financial expertise, or are you interested in his supernatural skills? Of course, we have a total package deal at a discounted price."

"I'm not really sure," Granny said. "We want to ask him a few questions."

"Well, have a seat and I'll see if he can fit you in," Tim said as he steered his chair back through the narrow door from which he'd come. When he finally disappeared through it, there were more loud crashes, then shouts from another, angry voice.

"Tim Cratchit! Do you have any idea how much a box of crystal balls costs these days? I didn't buy you that mechanical chair so you could race through the store trashing everything."

"Sorry, boss," Tim shouted back. "You've got customers . . . and they're breathers!"

Suddenly, the door flew open and a thin, wiry old man in a

black suit hurried into the room. His white, bushy hair stood up in all directions, almost as if he had been repeatedly scared out of his wits.

"So, who was next?" he said with a broad smile.

Everyone in the waiting room said, "Me!"

"Only the living people, people!" Scrooge bellowed.

"That would be us," Granny said, taking the opportunity to usher the girls and Mr. Canis forward.

"Excellent," the old man said as he gestured for the group to follow him into the back. They had to wait for Tim to get out of the doorway, but once this was accomplished, they found themselves in a room decorated in ruby red and midnight blue tapestries, with fluffy pillows scattered on the floor and incense burning in a small pot on a shelf. In the middle of the room was a round table surrounded by six high-backed chairs. Scrooge invited everyone to sit down and then did so himself.

"I apologize for that mob scene. I hired Tim to keep them out, but I think the boy is in over his head," he continued. "Ghosts can be quite a handful."

"Ghosts!" Sabrina said with a laugh.

If the man heard the doubt in her voice, he ignored it.

"They're like mice. I can't get rid of them. Ever since that business with Christmas, all the spirits on the astral plane feel it's their duty to come and show me how I've ruined the holidays of everyone I know. I'll admit, I was a pain at Christmastime, but I think I've turned it around. Doesn't seem to matter to the Ghosts of Easter, Passover, Thanksgiving, Yom Kippur, the anniversary of the Boxer Rebellion, Bastille Day, National Donut Day, Lincoln's Birthday, and the anniversary of the Woodstock concert. The whole thing has gotten ridiculous. How many Arbor Days could I have ruined? Not to mention Kwanzaa and Causal Fridays. It got so bad that I was fired from my job at the bank. It's really difficult to approve home loans with the Ghost of Earth Day Future walking around turning off all the office computers to save energy."

Scrooge bent under the table and returned with a calculator and a crystal ball. "OK, let's get down to business. We do two things here: finances and phantoms. What's it going to be?"

Granny reached into her handbag and removed the business card Sabrina had found in her mother's wallet. Scrooge took it, flipped it over, and then smiled.

"Ah, Veronica," he said wistfully. "Where did you get this?"

"She's our mom," Daphne said.

The man grinned. "Your mother is a saint. She helped me get the lease on this store when I decided to go into business for myself. She's lovely. Just lovely! I miss her dearly."

"She's in Ferryport Landing," Granny Relda said. "I'm her mother-in-law. We've come to understand that Veronica was well-known in the Everafter community."

"Community, huh? If that's what you want to call it. Yes, she helped us out, all of us. I'm glad to hear she's all right. She vanished, and there were rumors she was killed. I didn't believe it for a second. I was sure her spirit would stop by if it were true."

"We're investigating the death of another spirit. King Oberon was murdered, and we were hoping you might—"

"Of course!" Scrooge said, cutting off Granny Relda. "Everybody grab hands and close your eyes."

"This is a waste of time," Moth mumbled.

"Mr. Scrooge, we aren't here to talk to his ghost," the old woman said.

"Oh?"

"We were hoping you might be able to give us some information. Anything you might know about who would want to kill the king."

Scrooge laughed. "Well, you don't need a psychic for that. Everyone wanted to kill the king. I wanted to kill the king. He was a jerk—"

"—azoid," Daphne finished.

"He was an arrogant, stupid bully," Scrooge continued. "He sent his goons down here once a week to collect his taxes, but what did any of us ever get out of it? Zip! Nothing! Jack squat! It was extortion money if you ask me. It's a wonder someone didn't kill him before—"

"Did you attend yesterday's meeting?" Mr. Canis interrupted.

"No. I have no patience for all that clucking, and I'm not talking about the chickens. They all run around talking about rebuilding the kingdom, but nothing ever gets done," Scrooge said. "Not that it makes a difference to me, you see. I don't care if it ever happens. And don't expect me to help out. Why should I help build something the fairies are going to control? If you don't have wings, they look down their noses at you."

"How dare you!" Moth cried. "Hold your tongue, underling, or I will cut it out of your mouth."

"See what I mean? No respect," Scrooge grumbled.

"So you didn't support Oberon's plans," Granny said.

"I like the idea of a homeland for Everafters, even one that's hidden, but it has to be democratic. I don't want to be ruled by a king—been there, done that. Lots of folks feel the same, but Oberon never listened to us. I think the concept of elections made him nervous. He fought anyone with a different idea, and then the whole conversation turned into an argument. Plus, they never could agree on a place to put the Greenery. Right now, it's in the park, but before that it was downtown, and then up in Harlem, and then over in Brooklyn. They're talking about moving it again, out to Newark, New Jersey. Well, they can forget ever seeing Scrooge on that side of the river. An Everafter has to have standards."

"We should go. This is clearly a dead end," Moth snapped.

"A dead end is exactly what it is. You read the sign on the door, right? You people aren't getting it, are you? Here, take my hand," Scrooge said, clutching Sabrina's in his own. "Now, close your eyes. We have to concentrate to get Oberon's attention."

"What on earth are you doing?" Moth demanded.

"Shhhh!"

"Is this going to give me nightmares?" Daphne whispered, taking Scrooge's other hand.

"Depends . . . was his head chopped off or anything like that? They often come back looking the way they did when they died."

"He was poisoned," Granny Relda said, sounding a little uneasy.

"Should be fine. He might be a little green. Still, I have to warn you. Even if we see Oberon, he'll be difficult to understand. I think it has something to do with the amount of energy the spooks use to become visible. For some reason, it's more important to be seen than heard, so they trade the language for the body. Sometimes I can make out what they want to say by having them play charades. Now, let's concentrate. Oberon? Oberon, are you there?"

Sabrina rolled her eyes. "You're just going to call out his name? It's that easy?"

"Fine, if you want the whole shebang there's no extra charge," Scrooge said as he flipped a switch on the wall. Rays of light shot out of the crystal ball, speckling the tapestries with shimmering suns, moons, and stars. The sound of a powerful wind came from speakers mounted on the ceiling. Scrooge reached under the table and pulled out a huge swami hat. It was bright purple and had a shiny red ruby in its center. He plopped it on his head. "This authentic enough for you?"

Sabrina scowled.

"Oberon, King of the Fairies. We call on you. Come forth and reveal yourself," Scrooge continued. Unfortunately, his request went unanswered and the family sat waiting for several minutes. "I'm sorry. He might be on another line."

"I'm leaving!" Moth said and started to stand. "Nothing good can come from snooping in the afterworld."

Granny snatched her by the sleeve and pulled her back into her seat. "Be patient," she scolded.

"Come out, come out wherever you are. That's right, Your Majesty, we're having a party and you're invited," Scrooge sang.

For once, Sabrina agreed with Moth. She was sure Scrooge was a scam artist and was preparing to march out of the room herself when an odd chill crept up her spine. She felt as if she were coming down with a horrible head cold. In fact, her whole body felt weird, almost as if it were filled with stuffing, like she had become a giant teddy bear.

"Granny, what's going on?" Sabrina asked as the hair on her arms stood on end.

"I think he's here," Scrooge said, sounding relieved. "Oberon, is that you?"

Sabrina's mouth opened on its own, and a ghostly voice boomed out of it. "Where am I?"

"Hey! Did that come out of me?" Sabrina cried, looking at her sister, who stared at her with eyes as wide as moons. Even Moth looked frightened.

"Wowzers!" Scrooge said to Sabrina. "You're a natural medium. Your mother has the same ability!"

Sabrina couldn't respond. The ghost had full possession of her now.

"Where am I?" the voice asked. This time Sabrina's arms flailed around as if she were angry.

"Your . . . Your Majesty?" Moth sputtered. Her eyes were huge and frightened.

Scrooge bit his lip. "Oberon, I have some bad news for you. Are you sitting down?"

"Yes," Oberon's voice said. "Wait! Where's my body?"

"Yeah, that's the bad news. You're dead."

There was a long silence, but Sabrina could still feel the king's presence inside of her. Suddenly, her mouth opened again and a single frustrated word came out.

"Fudge."

"I know. It's a real bummer. Right now, you're stuck in limbo,

and you're going to stay there until your killer is brought to justice. Luckily, we've got some people here who want to help you out with that inconvenience."

"King Oberon, it is I, your loyal subject, Moth. I have been caring for Puck since you departed," the little fairy bragged as she hefted Puck's chrysalis onto the table. "He is here with me."

"I know, I can smell him from the astral plane," Oberon groaned, then forced Sabrina's body to walk over to Puck's chrysalis. Sabrina felt her hand move over it, caressing the cocoon lightly. She could feel a wave of regret pour over her, an odd sensation considering how Oberon had reacted when he discovered Puck in his office. Hadn't he called his son a traitor? Sabrina's anger gave her the strength to wrench back control of her body.

"Sabrina, don't fight him. We need to ask him some important questions," Granny said.

"Easy for you to say. There's only one person in your body," Sabrina snapped.

"We'll try to make this quick. Oberon, do you have any idea who killed you?" Granny Relda asked.

"Cobweb!" the voice bellowed as Oberon took control again. "He poisoned me. He brought me a glass of wine to celebrate the arrival of Veronica's girls. A moment after he left, I felt faint and collapsed. There was a terrible pain and then blackness."

"Of course. I knew it all along!" Moth exclaimed.

"Do you know why he wanted to kill you?" Granny asked Oberon.

"No," the king said. "He's the last person I would have suspected. Oh, I am so angry! I had Mets season tickets. What a waste!"

"Are you sure it was Cobweb?" Mr. Canis said.

"I think I know who killed me!" Oberon roared.

"When someone murders a king, it's usually to take the throne for themselves," Canis responded. "Puck is the heir, yet Cobweb gave him medical attention. He saved the boy's life. It doesn't make sense."

"Perhaps there's someone else you've offended?" Granny Relda asked.

"That's ridiculous, you stupid woman! Everyone loves me!"

"What about your wife? We saw you fighting with her," Granny replied, brushing off the insult.

"The queen? Sure, we fight, but you try being married for five thousand years and see if you don't bicker."

"Whoever did it is a member of the Scarlet Hand," Sabrina said. "Have you had any run-ins with them?"

"The Scarlet what?" Oberon asked. "I've never heard of a Scarlet Hand. I'm telling you, it had to be Cobweb. He's the last person I saw. He brought me a glass of wine. It had poison in it. I died. I think this case is closed."

Suddenly, the chill in Sabrina's body disappeared and a new

voice came from her mouth. "Please insert fifty cents for an additional ten minutes."

"Sorry, we've lost the connection," Scrooge said.

"Well, get him back!" Moth demanded.

"Oberon? Your Majesty?" Scrooge called out. "I'm sorry. He's gone. I hope it was helpful."

Granny stood up and shook the old man's hand. "It was more than helpful. We now know how Cobweb killed Oberon. All we have to do is track him down and turn him in. If only detective work were always this easy."

"Forget detective work," Scrooge said. "Sabrina could make a bundle as a psychic."

Sabrina scowled.

Scrooge led them to the lobby, where Tim was struggling with his scooter again. When he was situated they paid Scrooge's fee.

"Satisfied customers, eh? Well, well, that's good news," Tim said as he counted the bills. "I was a big fan of your mother, by the way. She was good people."

Daphne rested her elbows on the desk and smiled brightly.

"Would you say it for me?" she asked.

"Say what?"

"You know! The line," the little girl begged.

Tim frowned, rolled his eyes, and took a deep breath. "God bless us, every one," he grumbled.

Daphne clapped her hands and giggled like she'd just stumbled into a surprise party.

"I should start charging for that," Tim muttered.

"So, what do we do now?" Sabrina asked when the group stepped back out into the blustery street.

"Mustardseed wants us to report everything to Oz," Granny said as she hailed a cab. "I'm hoping he might also be able to help us find Cobweb."

"Where to, folks?" the cabbie asked as his car pulled to the curb.

"Macy's department store," Granny said, as she helped the girls into the taxi.

"I'm not feeling myself," Mr. Canis said from the sidewalk. "Can you manage without me?"

Granny nodded. "Do you need a ride?"

Mr. Canis looked around and shook his head. "I think a walk in the cold air will be good for me."

Granny waved good-bye, and the taxi headed north toward Macy's.

Daphne clapped her hands. "We're off to see the Wizard."

Sabrina rolled her eyes. "You've been waiting all day to say that, haven't you?"

Daphne grinned from ear to ear.

When they arrived at Macy's, a huge crowd of people was pushing its way into the store at the same time that an equally huge crowd was trying to get out. Sabrina was not surprised. Christmas Eve was just three days away, and what would the holidays be without thousands of panicked shoppers scrambling for last-minute gifts? Macy's was always packed at this time of the season—not only for the shopping, but also because of its legendary window displays. Crowds gazed at each window, featuring scenes from different holiday stories. This year the displays featured *The Night Before Christmas*, *A Christmas Carol*, and *The Nutcracker*. Each was more magical than the last, with automated characters moving as fluidly as human beings.

Granny urged them all to hold hands as they moved through the crowd.

"Mommy!" a small child cried as he pointed at Puck's chrysalis. "I want that for Christmas!"

Sabrina snickered to herself, imagining Puck's stinky cocoon underneath a Christmas tree. She would have loved to see Puck's face when he crawled out of it and found a strange little boy staring at him.

"So, did Oz say what he does at the store?" Daphne yelled above the crowd.

"No, but I'm sure if we ask, someone will help us find him," Granny Relda said. "He's a bit of a character. Everyone must know him."

"No need. I found him," Moth said, nodding at one of the many huge picture windows that ran along the sides of building.

Oz was behind the glass, working on a window display featuring several elves assembling toys in a red-and-green factory. One, however, had gone haywire. It was pounding on the head of its robot colleague with a wooden mallet. Oz stepped through the chaos, aiming his silver remote at the malfunctioning elf but having little effect. Sabrina remembered that L. Frank Baum, the man who had documented the history of the land of Oz, described the Wizard as a mechanical genius, able to build frighteningly realistic creations. In the stories, Oz managed to convince the entire fairy land that he was a powerful sorcerer, but today he looked foolish. The throngs of people were as amused by the Wizard's antics as they were by his creations. A few grown-ups laughed loudly, especially when the rogue elf smacked him in the shin with his hammer.

Granny maneuvered through the crowd to tap on the window. Oz turned with a scowl, but it disappeared when he spotted her. He waved her inside and then climbed out of the back of the window display.

The group pushed their way into the bustling store, where Oz was waiting. He ushered everyone into a room marked STAFF ONLY. What Sabrina saw inside was even more amazing than the window displays. The room was filled with half-finished robots, many blinking and buzzing, waiting for their moment in the spotlight. Automated birds sat on perches singing sweet little songs, and a family of half-painted polar bears played with a newborn cub in the corner. They looked so lifelike that Sabrina couldn't help feeling nervous, worrying the bears might turn on her at any moment.

Oz's workroom was stacked high with papers and old engineering books. A full-length mirror leaned against a wall, and a thin cot sat in the far corner. Sabrina suspected the Wizard slept in here more often than not.

"I'm sorry. I'm so frazzled," Oz said as he pushed unfinished projects off chairs to make room for the family. "Today is 'what happened to the rest of the year?' day here at the store. People seem to forget there are three hundred sixty-four days to shop before Christmas."

"We were admiring your windows," Granny said. "The displays are extraordinary. Everything moves like it's alive. How do you do it?"

Oz picked up a robot head. It blinked and smiled at him. "A good magician never reveals his tricks. I used to be a first-rate sleight-of-hand man back in the day. When I first found myself in Oz, I did a disappearing coin trick for the Mayor of Munchkinland, and before I knew it, I was the Great and Terrible Oz! Unfortunately, there aren't a lot of jobs in New York City for ex-wizards. I tried my hand entertaining at kids' birthday parties, but video games put an end to that, of course. When I heard the store needed help with its displays, I jumped at the opportunity. I always had a knack for gizmos and gadgets. Funnily enough, I'm still creating illusions after all this time. And, believe me, the robots in that window are a lot harder to rule than the Land of Oz ever was. Now, I know you all didn't come down here just to admire the decorations. How goes the search?"

"We've got a suspect," Daphne said.

Oz raised an eyebrow.

"Cobweb," Granny said.

"That's impossible," Oz said.

"Oberon told us," Moth snapped.

The Wizard raised both eyebrows.

"It's a long story," Granny said. "We believe Cobweb has been working with a group called the Scarlet Hand."

"That mark they found on Oberon's body," Oz said.

Granny nodded. "Can you pass this information on to Mustardseed? He may be in danger from Cobweb as well."

"Of course," Oz said.

"Unfortunately, that brings us to another dead end. We don't know where to find Cobweb. He's not at the Golden Egg, is he?"

"No. All but Titania, Mustardseed, and his men have scattered."

"Does he have any friends?" Granny Relda asked.

The Wizard shook his head. "He was pretty busy following Oberon's and Titania's orders. He was very loyal to them. That's what makes this all such a big surprise. Still, there might be someone who can help. There's a fairy godmother over in Midtown West who I've seen with Cobweb. If he needs a place to hide, he might head there. Her name is Twilarose. She owns some kind of dress shop."

"That's a big help," Daphne said.

"By the way," Oz said, "between me and you, your friend—the chubby guy . . ."

"Mr. Hamstead?" Sabrina asked.

"Yes. He made himself a powerful enemy today. Word is he stole Fat Tony's girlfriend. If I were him, I'd get out of town as fast as possible. A fairy godfather isn't the type of person you cross."

Twilarose's Fashion Emporium was on the corner of Eleventh Avenue and Fifty-seventh Street next to a parking lot for garbage trucks. The smell on the block was even worse than the one coming from Puck's cocoon.

Granny had left word at the hotel for Mr. Hamstead and Bess to meet them at the dress shop. They arrived soon after the Grimms and Moth, though they were so caught up in conversation, they barely noticed the family waiting for them in the fading daylight. Granny pulled them aside and gave them Oz's warning. Bess looked concerned, but Mr. Hamstead just smiled and reminded Granny Relda that he was more than capable of taking care of himself and Bess, if need be.

While the grown-ups talked, Sabrina looked at the store's window display and decided that this Twilarose person wasn't exactly sure what the word *fashion* meant. The dresses were so gaudy and ill-fitting that the mannequins wearing them looked embarrassed.

"So what's the difference between a fairy and a fairy god-mother?" Daphne asked Moth.

The little fairy sneered. "Of course an ignoramus like you wouldn't know the difference. Fairy godmothers and godfathers are lower beings. Unlike true-blood fairies, they need wands to perform magic. And they are born as adults, sometimes as very old people. They can be painfully ugly, with gray hair and wrinkles."

"It must take great strength on your part to tolerate them," said Granny Relda sarcastically. She had caught the end of Moth's speech.

"It does indeed," Moth said, nodding earnestly.

"We don't know this Twilarose or her loyalties. If she's hiding Cobweb, she might be dangerous," Hamstead said, pulling his pants up over his belly. "Be careful, and keep your eyes peeled."

A fat, orange tomcat lay outside, blocking the entrance to the store. Granny shooed it away, and it raced yowling into an old re-frigerator box someone had dragged out onto the sidewalk. When the path was clear, Granny pushed open the door.

Inside the shop were racks and racks of shiny, poofy-sleeved ballroom dresses, covered in frills and lace. There were so many in the small shop that Sabrina felt like they were pushing in on her from every side. Several shelves of shoes in shocking, unnatural colors lined the walls, as well as a case displaying a collection of funky-shaped handbags.

A roly-poly lady stepped out of the back room and stood behind the counter. She had a big, blue beehive hairdo atop an almost perfect circle of a head. Her eyebrows were drawn on, and her cheeks and lips were bright pink. She was wearing a baby blue satin dress that made her look as if she might be off to her senior prom at any moment. A rhinestone belt with blue-and-green blinking lights completed the look.

"Welcome to Twilarose's Fashion Emporium. How can I help you?" the woman sang. "We're having a sale on spring-fling formalwear and shoes. It's never too early to get a head start on the coming seasons. And remember, everything in this store is a Twilarose original. I design all the clothes myself."

"So you're Twilarose?" Granny asked.

"The one and only," the old woman said. "Perhaps you've seen my work on the runways of Milan, Paris, and Canton, Ohio."

"I'm Daphne Grimm. The Wizard of Oz sent us," Daphne announced.

Twilarose's eyes grew wide. "Indeed. Oh my! I heard the Grimm family was in town," she said, louder than necessary. "I'm so glad no one in the Grimm family was hurt in that riot at the Golden

Egg. Terrible, terrible situation. I'm so thrilled to meet the Grimm family."

"I was going to ask if you had seen Cobweb, but it's pretty clear he's hiding in the back," Sabrina said. The woman was obviously trying to warn him of their arrival and she wasn't being subtle about it at all.

"I'm not sure what you're talking about, you people in the Grimm family! I just make clothing. In fact, I feel inspired. I'm going to give you all the Twilarose VIP Makeover! Won't that be fun?"

Twilarose reached into the folds of her dress and produced a magic wand with a star on the end. Sabrina recognized it immediately as a fairy godmother wand. She'd used one herself not too long ago. Twilarose waved it in the air and there was a loud *bam!*

When Sabrina looked down, she was wearing a puffy, leopard-print dress with matching shoes. She looked over at the others and saw their clothes had been replaced as well. Daphne wore a rainbow-colored cancan dress, and Granny Relda was in a big pink gown with a hat as large as her whole body. Moth and Bess were both dressed in tracksuits covered in little golden bells. They clomped around in snowshoes. Each of them was covered in so much makeup it appeared to have been applied by a paintball gun.

Even poor Mr. Hamstead had not escaped the magical makeover. He was now wearing an electric blue tuxedo with tails and a top hat. And Puck's cocoon was draped in multicolored ribbons.

Twilarose clapped her hands. "Voila! I am brilliant!" she shouted. "You are all the toast of New York City thanks to me."

"You fool! We don't have time for this nonsense," Moth said. "Give us Cobweb!"

"You don't like the outfits? Perhaps something more work appropriate will please you." The fairy godmother waved her wand again, and—*bam!*—the dresses were gone, replaced with even more outrageous outfits. Now Granny, Sabrina, Daphne, Moth, and Bess each wore a long evening gown and a badge, with handcuffs and a billy club swinging from a belt. Mr. Hamstead wore a black-and-white prison uniform. A ball and chain was shackled to his left leg. He looked down and grunted.

"*C'est magnifique!*" Twilarose said. "But the makeup is all wrong."

*Bam!*

Sabrina turned to the mirror. She looked like a geisha from outer space, with white pancake makeup and silver lipstick.

*Bam!*

Now she was wearing fake vampire teeth and a beanie cap with a propeller on top.

*Bam!*

Sabrina looked down to find she was carrying a toy poodle

with a diamond collar; she had two purple shiners and some of her teeth had been blacked out.

Moth stepped forward and waved an angry finger at Twilarose. "I am a fairy and a member of the royal court, making me your superior, so if you are quite finished with your atrocious fashion show—"

"Atrocious?" Twilarose cried. She flicked her wand, and before anyone could stop her, they were all bound from head to toe in thick steel chains.

"It has been a long time since the glory days of Cinderella, but I'd hardly call my work atrocious."

"Whoa, whoa, whoa!" Daphne exclaimed. "You're Cinderella's fairy godmother?"

"Yes. She made me a fashion design icon. After that dress, every princess from here to Timbuktu would have killed for one of my designs."

"Enough!" Moth roared as she wiggled free. "Your blabbering is wasting our time. If you don't tell us where Cobweb is, I'll—"

"There is no need for threats, Moth," a voice said from behind the curtains at the back of the store. The drapes were pulled aside and Cobweb stepped through.

"Murderer!" Moth screamed.

"I have killed no one."

"We know you did it!" Sabrina said. "We heard it straight from Oberon."

Just then, there was a tremendous crash and the front door to the shop blew off its hinges. The group struggled to see what had caused the commotion. Standing in the doorway were Fat Tony and Bobby. Their magic wands were held tight in their huge hands.

"How did you find us?" Bess demanded.

The two goons ignored her. Their eyes were locked on Mr. Hamstead.

"You shouldn't have messed with my girl," Fat Tony said as he and his partner stepped into the store. "'Cause now, you and me . . . we're going to have to settle this the way we did back in the old days."

Fat Tony raised his wand and, with a flick of his wrist, a bolt of white-hot energy rocketed toward the group.

# 6

**H**AMSTEAD LEAPED OUT OF THE WAY, MISSING the blast by inches. Unfortunately, it crashed into a rack of polyester dresses that exploded into flames.

"My spring collection!" Twilarose shouted as she desperately tried to put out the fire melting her gowns. She stomped feverishly on a pink, hoopskirted prom dress, completely ignoring the peril of everyone around her.

In the chaos, Sabrina watched Cobweb fly out of the shop.

"Forget the dresses!" she yelled, as flames rapidly spread throughout the shop. "Get us out of these chains!"

Twilarose turned and flicked her wand, freeing the group. But they weren't out of danger. Smoke filled the room, blinding Fat Tony and Bobby. The two fairy godfathers shot their wands in every direction. Bobby's aim was lousy; each attack from his wand spiraled into unintended targets, causing the flames to double in a matter of seconds.

Sabrina rushed to rescue Puck's chrysalis from a nest of smoldering feather boas. Once she had it, she scrambled over to her family, who were hiding behind a rack of sequined capes.

"Where's Cobweb?" Daphne asked.

"He's gone," Sabrina said, ducking her head to avoid another magical blast. "We need to get out of here, too!"

"Bess!" Fat Tony bellowed over the chaos. "You're my girl, now and always."

Sabrina handed Puck's cocoon to Moth. "Can you get him to safety?"

"Of course," the fairy girl snapped. Her wings sprang from her back, and soon she and Puck were hovering above the floor. She zipped through the fairy godfathers' crossfire and soared through the open door. With so much smoke in the air, Fat Tony and Bobby didn't even notice their escape.

"Bess! Take my hand," Hamstead said.

"Don't worry, Ernie. I've got this one," Bess said. She took his hand and with the other reached behind her back for something in her backpack. Suddenly a flame shot out from the bottom, and she and her chubby new boyfriend were lifted right off the ground. Sabrina watched in amazement as they rocketed out of the store.

"Uh, I want one of those," Daphne said.

Twilarose went next, stumbling over a pyramid of tiaras before making it to the door.

"Our turn!" Sabrina snatched Daphne and Granny by the hand and raced across the room. By this time, Bobby and Fat Tony seemed to have gotten wise to what was happening. Their attacks came more quickly, and the Grimms had to race at full speed to get to the exit.

"Wait!" Daphne cried, pulling away from the group and rushing back into the chaos to retrieve something from the floor before rejoining her family.

Once outside, they stumbled onto the snowy sidewalk, gasping for air. Sabrina rubbed the soot out of her eyes and scanned the street. Twilarose was gone, as was Moth. Hamstead and Bess, however, were waiting outside, safe and sound.

"Where's Moth?" Sabrina asked.

"She flew that way," Hamstead said, pointing south.

"And there goes Cobweb," Granny said, pointing to the sky. The dark fairy was flapping his wings as hard as he could, flying in the opposite direction. "We have to catch him."

"Forget Cobweb," Sabrina said. "Moth has Puck!"

"She'll take care of him," Granny said. "We can't let Cobweb get away."

"Do you see that?" a woman cried, pointing at Cobweb. She was so surprised by the flying fairy she dropped her bag of groceries. Fruits and vegetables spilled out onto the pavement. "It's an angel!"

Granny frowned, reached into her handbag, and then blew forgetful dust all over the woman. Her eyes glazed over.

"You had a very boring day," Granny said.

"I did," the woman replied, then walked aimlessly away.

"We'll never catch him on foot," Granny said to the girls, whirling around in search of a cab. The street was packed with cars, but every taxi was already taken. Cobweb was going to escape, and there was nothing the family could do to stop him.

"I need something . . . like a pumpkin," Daphne said, scanning the street.

"What are you talking about?" Sabrina asked.

"Wait! This will work." Daphne reached down and snatched a zucchini the woman had left behind when Granny wiped her memory.

Sabrina watched Daphne place the zucchini back on the ground and then take a long, thin piece of wood out of her pocket—it was Twilarose's magic wand.

"This is what I went back for," the little girl explained. "Twilarose dropped it when she escaped."

"*Liebling*," Granny said. "Wands are dangerous."

"She's right," Hamstead said. "You could hurt yourself."

Daphne flicked her wrist and a bolt of energy blasted from the star at the end of the wand, leaving a trail of sparkles. The magic hit the zucchini, there was a blinding flash—and when Sabrina's eyes adjusted, the zucchini was still there.

"I don't understand. I watched her do it in the store." Daphne shook the wand vigorously. "I think we need to charge it."

But before the little girl even finished her sentence, the zucchini began to change. It grew, morphing and twisting, until it was as big as a car. Wheels appeared on its side, then bumpers on both ends and windows—and when the transformation was complete, the detectives were standing in front of an emerald green town car, complete with sunroof and spinning tire rims.

"Incredible," Granny Relda said.

"And it goes nicely in a salad," Daphne said proudly. "Now, all we need is a driver."

She searched the street and spotted the same orange tomcat that had been blocking their path only minutes ago. It hovered in a doorway, eyeing the group as if waiting to be fed. "I know it worked on some mice once. Let's see if a cat is any different."

She waved the wand again, and the sparkly blast shot the cat straight into the air. It let out a surprised yowl and then, just like the zucchini, began to morph. In no time at all, the tabby became a young, redheaded man wearing a black suit and a little leather cap.

"What's your name?" Daphne asked.

"Chester," the driver said.

"We need you to follow a flying fairy," Bess said.

"Now there's a sentence you don't hear every day," Chester said. He pushed a button on a keychain he was holding and the car's alarm deactivated. Then he rushed to open the doors and helped everyone inside. He hopped into the front seat.

"Buckle up," Chester said, slamming his foot on the gas. The car roared down the street after Cobweb.

Chester zipped around cars and pedestrians like a professional racecar driver. Sabrina quickly fastened her seat belt, then craned her neck out the window in hopes of spotting their target. She didn't have to search for long. Cobweb was directly in front of them, darting in and out of traffic.

Unfortunately, as Sabrina discovered when she peeked out the rear window, they were being followed, too. Fat Tony and Bobby were in pursuit and firing magical rockets at them. One hit a nearby fire hydrant and it exploded, sending a geyser of water high into the air.

"Here comes the goon squad," Hamstead warned.

"Don't worry, folks," Chester said. He made a quick left and then a right, losing the fairy godfathers and beating a couple of lights until an unfortunate turn landed them in bumper-to-bumper traffic. Sabrina watched Cobweb soar overhead with ease. Meanwhile, Chester sat in the front seat, licking the back of his hand. She'd almost forgotten he was a cat.

"Can you open the sunroof?" Daphne asked.

"Sure can," Chester said, and the sunroof slid back, exposing the passengers to the sky.

"*Liebling*, are you thinking what I'm thinking? Because if you are—"

"Don't worry, Granny. I'm good at this," Daphne replied, then stood up so that her head was sticking out of the roof. "It's all in the wrist."

Daphne sent a flash of magic toward the traffic in front of them. Cars were suddenly jerked to the sides of the road as if by some mighty, invisible hand. When the way was clear, Chester stomped on the gas pedal and they were off once again.

"You're going to get hurt," Sabrina said as she pulled Daphne back into the car.

"You're not the boss of me," Daphne snapped.

Chester raced into Times Square and came to a screeching halt when a crowd of pedestrians stepped out into the intersection. Cobweb soared over the tourists' heads, but no one noticed. They were all too distracted by the dizzying lights and sights of Broadway. The dark fairy nosedived into a subway station and disappeared.

"Sorry. I can't take the car down there," Chester said.

The group climbed out of the car just as Fat Tony and Bobby reappeared, firing wildly once again. Hamstead and Bess leaped out of the way of an incoming blast, which hit a stop sign instead and transformed it into a monkey. The monkey shrieked and disappeared into the crowd.

Daphne turned on the goons and fired a return volley. It hit both Fat Tony and Bobby dead on, and in a flash their feet were encased in concrete. With their wings unable to keep the extra weight aloft, the men crashed to the ground. Their wands tumbled out of their hands and fell into an open sewer grate.

"Hey! I'm pretty good with this thing!" Daphne cheered as she waved her wand in the air. Granny quickly snatched it out of her hand and gave it to Chester.

"Would you be a dear and give this back to Twilarose?"

Chester nodded. "Sure. Can I keep the car?"

Daphne grumbled as the former cat drove away, but she didn't dwell on it, instead leading the charge down the subway steps after Cobweb. Sabrina helped Granny Relda down the steps and caught glimpses of Cobweb in the busy station, pushing through the crowds. He removed something from his pocket and swiped it at the subway turnstile, hurrying to the platform just as a train pulled into the station.

The family rushed to the turnstile, but without fare cards they were denied entry. Granny called out to Cobweb, and the fairy turned to face her.

"I didn't do it," he said.

"If you're innocent then you will have a chance to prove it when you go to trial," Granny said.

"There is no justice in the kingdom. There are no courts, no juries. I would be tried and convicted by Titania herself. My head would be in the Hudson River by sunup."

Cobweb stepped into the train. Helpless, the family could only watch as it disappeared into the tunnel.

"He's getting away," Sabrina said.

"I know," the old woman said. "And we're letting him."

Ↄↄ

Granny ushered everyone into a nearby coffee shop and ordered hot chocolate for the entire group. Once the steaming cups were delivered, she rushed off to make a phone call.

Sabrina couldn't help worrying. Things were getting dangerous, and Daphne was throwing herself into the middle of it all. Plus, Moth had raced off with Puck and could be anywhere in the city by now.

When Granny returned, brushing snow off her coat, she was eager to leave. "All right, everyone, let's go," she said.

"Where are we going?" Daphne asked.

"To see Titania," the old woman said.

"What?" Sabrina cried. "She tried to kill us!"

Granny smiled. "I remember, *liebling*."

Night had fallen by the time they reached Central Park. They found the Hans Christian Andersen statue, waited while a dark-haired woman walking a little white West Highland terrier passed out of sight, then said the magic words. As before, the Golden Egg was immediately revealed.

The damage to the restaurant from the previous night was gone. Except for a few broken chairs in the corner, there was no sign of the disturbance at all. The place was empty except for a cat playing Irish jigs on a fiddle. Momma was behind the bar washing some glasses.

"Good to see you, folks," she said. "Care for something to eat? The kitchen's open."

"No, thank you," Granny said. "We're meeting Titania here."

The woman sighed. "And I just got this place cleaned up."

"Which Everafter are you?" Daphne asked.

The woman smiled. "Mother Goose in the flesh—or in this case, in the feather." Suddenly, she transformed into a large black goose with a blue bonnet on her head. Daphne clapped, and the goose changed back into the bartender.

"It's nice to meet members of Veronica's family," Momma said as she washed glasses. "I was so busy with customers, I didn't get a chance to talk to you the other night. I knew Wilhelm and Jacob pretty well. Nice guys. They were always trying to help. I guess it runs in the family. Veronica was the same way."

Sabrina sat down on a barstool. "You knew my mother?"

Momma nodded. "Oh, yes. Sweet lady. She helped me get into bartending school. Without her, I'd still be living at the Sunshine Hotel on Bowery."

"The Sunshine Hotel?" Granny asked.

"Yeah, it's a flophouse, one of those pay-by-the-day places. Real classy," Momma said sarcastically. "A few Everafters still live there—the ones who can afford the rent."

"And the others?"

"They make do in shelters. Some of them live on the street."

"But you're magical beings," Sabrina said. "Why would you live in such terrible conditions? You don't have to."

"Kiddo, just 'cause I can turn into a goose doesn't mean I don't have bills to pay. It ain't easy being an Everafter. None of us have identification. We can't get driver's licenses because eventually people are going to notice we aren't getting older. Signing a lease on an apartment without any credit history is impossible. Why, you can't even get a job without a social security number.

"Technically none of us exist. That's why Veronica was so well liked. She helped us find ways to work around the humans' rules. She cut the red tape when it was possible. Before she disappeared, she told me she was working on a plan that would help us help ourselves. She was going to give a big speech—but then, all of a sudden, she was gone."

Just then, Titania, Mustardseed, and Moth appeared. Mustardseed stood close to his mother, holding her hand, and Moth carried Puck's chrysalis in her arms. Titania's heartbreak was plain on her face.

"This old woman is completely incompetent," Moth sneered. "We had Cobweb within our grasp and she let him go, my queen."

"You say another bad thing about my granny, and you're going to get socked in the nose," Daphne threatened, then turned to Mr. Hamstead. "What does *incompetent* mean?"

"She's saying that your grandmother isn't any good at her job," Hamstead replied.

Daphne shot the fairy girl another nasty look.

"So you don't need me to help with the big words anymore?" Sabrina asked, trying not to sound too hurt.

"I never said I didn't need you. I just can't count on you," the little girl answered.

Before Sabrina could argue, Moth started another tirade.

"The whole lot of them are morons at best, Your Majesty. They put the prince and me into mortal danger, but only after we wandered around the entire city looking for clues. You should send them all away."

"I think that's enough, Moth," Mustardseed said. "You are exhausting my mother."

Moth scowled but held her tongue.

"Oz said you needed to speak to us," Mustardseed continued. He was so serious and mature. Sabrina studied his face, looking for signs that he was truly Puck's brother. They shared the same mouth and nose—but that was about it.

"Yes. This is difficult to say, but we can no longer help you solve Oberon's murder," Granny Relda said.

"What?" Daphne cried. Even Sabrina was surprised by her grandmother's words.

"Why?" Titania demanded.

"We were told that Cobweb killed your husband," Granny said. "But Cobweb claims he is innocent."

"Cobweb is lying!" Titania said.

"Maybe so," the old woman replied. "But he also says he cannot turn himself in because he would be executed immediately."

Mustardseed lowered his eyes.

"So it's true?" Granny said.

"Of course it's true!" Titania insisted. "Murderers reap what they sow. That is the way of my people."

"So he will not be given a trial? He won't have a chance to defend himself?" Granny Relda asked.

Titania raged. "You are just like Veronica! She was always forcing her beliefs about justice on the rest of us."

"Veronica and I obviously share the same sense of right and wrong."

Titania growled. "Cobweb killed my husband, and I will oversee his execution myself!"

"Then you will have to find him without our help," Granny said.

"I have never heard such treachery," Moth cried. "Who are you to tell us how to behave?"

"No! They're right. We will give him a trial," Mustardseed said.

"You are overstepping your authority!" Titania shouted at her son. "I am still queen."

"But there is no kingdom, Mother. It has been gone for years," Mustardseed said. "This is a different world, with different values. My father's bitter refusal to adapt is what broke us apart. Don't make the same mistakes. It's time to embrace our new home."

"You would throw away thousands of years of our history?" Titania asked.

"There is room for tradition," Mustardseed said. "But not traditions that rob us of justice. Sentencing someone to death because that is how it has always been done is wrong. If you believe all our old ways must be followed in this new world, then there is no hope that our community will ever unite. You will fail as Father did."

"Mustardseed!"

"Allow Cobweb to defend himself," Mustardseed said.

Titania stormed out of the room.

"I will make her understand," Mustardseed said. "Tell Cobweb he will be treated fairly."

Granny regarded the young fairy for a moment, then nodded. "Then we are back on the case."

Mustardseed turned to Moth. "You will accompany them."

"Your Highness!" Moth protested.

"Do it!" he bellowed before turning to leave the room. "This new justice is not in place yet. Don't forget what happens to those who refuse royalty."

"So, I guess we're back to the subway," Daphne said when he was gone.

"It's a place to start," said Granny. "Someone might have seen where Cobweb went."

"Or he may still be down there," said Momma, who had witnessed the whole conversation. "It's a good place to hide."

"We're going down into that filth?" Moth groaned.

"Great," Sabrina said. "Anyone got a flashlight and an extra two years? Do you know how many miles of subway track there are? Six hundred and fifty-six!" She recalled a report she had done in the fourth grade after a trip to the Transit Museum.

"That's only half your problem," said Momma. "The subway is also the kingdom of the six dwarfs."

Moth stamped her foot as if the news was more than she could tolerate.

Granny smiled. "And where can we find these dwarfs?"

The day had been long and far beyond exciting. Everyone agreed finding Cobweb could wait until the morning.

The group returned to the hotel to find Mr. Hamstead's room ransacked. His bed had been torn apart and his drawers rifled through. There was a note on the bathroom door that read:

*You can go back to Ferryport Landing dead or alive. Your choice.*

Hamstead snatched the note and crumpled it into a ball. "At least he gave me a choice," he said with a forced smile.

"Maybe I'm too much trouble for you," Bess said with a sigh.

Hamstead shook his head. "I've dealt with bigger threats than Fat Tony."

Bess gave him a big hug and a kiss on the cheek. "You take care, doll face. I'll see you bright and early in the morning."

"I hope we get invited to the wedding," Daphne sang after the blond beauty was gone.

Mr. Hamstead rolled his eyes but grinned from ear to ear. "I'm going to have the hotel put me in another room. You folks need to get some rest. The six dwarfs, if I remember them correctly, are a handful. We've got a big day tomorrow."

Granny led Sabrina, Moth, and Daphne back to their room. Moth propped Puck's chrysalis on the bed next to her and crawled under the covers. Sabrina lay next to her grandmother and sister in the other bed. She fell asleep listening to Daphne planning the former sheriff's wedding. She dreamed of doves flying out of the top of a wedding cake.

When Sabrina woke the next morning, she crawled out of bed and went into the bathroom hoping to combat her morning breath. She quietly shut the door, brushed her teeth, then washed her face. When she checked herself in the mirror, she screamed.

Hovering several feet off the ground behind her was Puck's funky cocoon. The top was split open, and something green and smelly was gurgling inside. When she turned around to get a better look, a pungent gas seeped out and filled her nose. It was the foulest smell Sabrina had ever experienced—like rotten cabbage, dirty laundry, and stinky cheese. She instinctively leaped back, but the sac followed her like a smelly puppy. She tried to maneuver around it, but the cocoon mimicked every step she took. She faked to the left and then to the right, only to have it block the bathroom door entirely, trapping her inside. That was when the real nightmare began.

A hissing sound not unlike a steam whistle filled Sabrina's ears and more of the gas blasted out of the top of the cocoon, filling the bathroom with a horrible fog. It seeped into her hair, into her socks—she could even taste it. She pinched her nose tightly, but it didn't help.

"Sabrina, are you okay in there?" her grandmother asked as she tapped on the door. "It seems as if your dinner isn't agreeing with you. Is there anything I can do? The hotel might have some antacids for your belly."

There was another knock on the door. "Hey! Light a match in there," Daphne shouted.

Suddenly, the door burst open and Moth shrieked in rage.

"How dare you!" she cried.

"My goodness gracious," Granny Relda said. "What is going on in here?"

"It just blew up on me," Sabrina cried as she pointed to the cocoon. It continued to spray her with mist, and there was no end in sight. "Make it stop!"

"What you've done is unforgivable!" Moth seethed. "You have stolen my right!"

"I didn't steal anything!" Sabrina insisted. "It followed me in here."

"Moth, what is happening?" Granny asked.

Moth growled. "During the larval stage, when a fairy is most vulnerable, he chooses the one person in the world he trusts the most to look after him. Once the choice is made, the vessel marks the person with a special scent, one the chrysalis can easily follow. It is a great honor, and it should have gone to me!"

"I didn't ask for this!" Sabrina cried.

"Well, then," Granny said as the last of the gas fizzed out of the top of the chrysalis. "I suppose congratulations are in order."

The smell was everywhere. No amount of washing could get it out. Sabrina took six showers, washed her hair, and scrubbed every inch of her body, but each time the smell returned with a vengeance. She could even smell it on her toothbrush. If she hadn't been so angry she might have cried.

Still, the smell was only half the nightmare. Sabrina discovered that wherever she went the cocoon followed, step for step. She shouted at it, hid from it, even threatened to drop kick it out the hotel window, but nothing would stop it. As she couldn't reasonably walk the streets with a flying, eggplant-shaped gas bomb hovering at her shoulder, Granny and Daphne went out in search of something that might work as camouflage.

Left alone with an angry Moth, Sabrina watched talk shows she was certain were inappropriate for her age. Moth stalked around the room with clenched fists, muttering bitter words under her breath.

"What's this?" Sabrina asked when her grandmother and sister returned with a long piece of string.

Granny tied one end of the string to the bottom of the cocoon and handed the other end to Sabrina. "Now, isn't that a lovely balloon?"

Sabrina grumbled. She felt like a grumpy child at the worst birthday party ever.

Mother Goose's directions were far better than any Bess or Oz had given the group. Momma knew exactly where to find the dwarfs. They lived in an abandoned subway station underneath the mayor's office downtown. The City Hall station had been closed decades ago, when new, longer subway cars made the platform impractical.

The walk to the station was especially cold, and the Grimms were glad to have scarves and mittens. Even Mr. Canis bought a big pair of gloves to hide his claws and a scarf to wrap around his whiskered head. Moth, Mr. Hamstead, and Bess didn't seem bothered by the cold at all—Moth because of her fairy blood, and Mr. Hamstead and Bess because they were too busy giggling and holding hands to notice the temperature.

The group crossed a small park and found the steel door in the sidewalk that Momma had told them led into the ancient subway station. Hardly anyone was out in the harsh weather, so it was easy to avoid being seen when Canis pulled the door open, revealing a flight of steps that led down into the darkness. Mr. Hamstead insisted that he go first, claiming his police training had prepared him for any kind of danger. It was obvious his boasting was for Bess's benefit, but Sabrina held her tongue.

Hamstead led the group down the steps, and when everyone was inside, Canis pulled the door closed. The loss of light blinded them.

"Creepy," Daphne said.

"Just be patient, *liebling*. Your eyes will adjust," Granny promised.

"Man, it smells foul down here," Bess said.

"I believe that is the girl," Canis said.

"Uh, hello? I'm standing right here!" Sabrina said.

Before long, their eyes did adjust, and Mr. Hamstead led them along a damp concrete passageway lined with huge pipes and electrical wiring. Every once in a while, the group would pass under a dingy, flickering lightbulb, which helped them see a few more feet ahead, but they were few and far between.

"We are getting close," Canis said, sniffing the air. "I smell them."

The tunnel opened into a huge station with an arched ceiling held up by elegant columns and cut through with skylights that allowed rays of light to shine down on the gold-tiled walls and floor. Sabrina had been in many subway stations in New York City, but this one was the most beautiful. The space felt like the lost tomb of a great pharaoh. At the center was a single train track where a lone subway car was parked.

"Hello?" Granny shouted. Her voice bounced off the walls and echoed back. "Is anyone here?"

"They have obviously abandoned this station," Moth said. "It's filthy and not fit for a dog. Even a thing as lowly as a dwarf couldn't live in such squalor."

Something flickered in the corner of Sabrina's vision. She spun quickly and thought she saw movement in the shadows along the far wall. She turned to Mr. Canis, whose senses were much more acute than hers. He held his finger to his lips to let her know he saw something, too, and to warn her to be quiet.

"What are we waiting for?" Moth continued as she headed for the train car. "We should take their train and search the tunnels ourselves."

Before she could step into the car, the station erupted with movement as five tiny men bore down on them, flipping and jumping, shouting and screaming. They stopped just short of the group, surrounding them like ninjas from a martial arts film.

The door to the subway car opened and a sixth little man with a long, white beard stepped out and eyed the group angrily through his round glasses. He wore a blue uniform jacket with a name patch on one pocket and a patch on the other that read MTA. Sabrina knew what the letters stood for—Metropolitan Transportation Authority. The little man worked for the subway.

"You're trespassing in the domain of the six dwarfs," he said, signaling to the others to close in on the group. "Trespassers get a beating. Invaders get death."

Sabrina watched as one of the little men slipped a set of brass knuckles on his hand.

Granny stepped forward. "We're not here to invade your territory."

A second dwarf clenched his fists. He had greasy half-moon spectacles on his nose. "These are our tunnels," he said. "We'll fight every one of you, chickadee!"

Mr. Canis growled. Sabrina could see he was losing his patience again.

"We're looking for someone, and we were told you could help," Sabrina said quickly. "A fairy flew down here last night. We think he's hiding in the tunnels."

"A fairy!" shouted one of the dwarfs in horror. "No fairies in the subway! Your kind isn't welcome here."

"We're not fairies," Daphne said. "Well, except for her," she added, pointing at Moth. "We're Grimms. We're detectives."

Suddenly, the white-bearded leader of the group cried out. "My oh my, it's you! It's Veronica's girls."

The little men immediately lowered their fists and smiled. They crowded around Sabrina and Daphne, offering up praise for their mother.

"Veronica was a gem."

"A real inspiration!"

"We loved her."

"What charisma!"

The men smiled and introduced themselves. Each had a different story about Sabrina and Daphne's mother. They all seemed to idolize her and regretted the day she had disappeared—the day of the "big speech." It was clear they thought the speech would have changed their lives in some way.

When it grew quiet again, the leader, who called himself Mr. One, spoke. "What are you doing down here?"

"We're looking for Cobweb," Daphne replied. "We're trying to arrest him."

"Just like your mother," Mr. One said with a chuckle.

"What do you mean by that?" Sabrina demanded.

"Veronica was always taking on other people's troubles. She wanted to help, even when it put her in some sticky situations. The woman was fearless. Anything we can do to help you would be an honor."

"We think Cobweb went underground," Hamstead said.

"Nobody knows these tunnels better than you do," Bess added, and the dwarfs puffed up with pride at her compliment.

"What do you say, boys?" Mr. One asked his companions. "Up for a fairy hunt?" He pronounced the word *fairy* as one might the word *rat*. Sabrina was starting to understand that dwarfs and fairies weren't fond of one another.

"Can we keep the train windows open?" Mr. Two asked, pointing his thumb at Sabrina. "Someone's a little funky."

Sabrina scowled.

The dwarfs ushered the group onto their subway car. Mr. One stepped inside the control room at the front of the car as the rest of the dwarfs hurried into their own positions. Mr. Two and Mr. Six made sure everyone got into a comfortable seat while Mr. Five and Mr. Three opened a couple of panels on the train's walls. Inside each panel was a bright yellow handle. The dwarfs each pulled one down, and suddenly there was a loud hiss and the train doors closed. Mr. One's voice came over the loudspeaker. "All passengers, welcome to the D train. Please, no eating, drinking, or playing loud music while onboard. Next stop . . . well, I guess we're just going to have to see. All right, everyone. Hold onto something! We're going express."

The train car suddenly surged forward, sending the little men tumbling and skidding across the floor. Sabrina and Daphne helped them to their feet, then grabbed onto the pole in the center of the car to steady themselves. The sisters looked out the windows and saw they were rocketing through the subway tunnels.

"You wouldn't happen to know a Mr. Seven, would you?" Daphne asked Mr. Two.

"We know him. He's our brother," the dwarf said.

Mr. Three frowned. "Next time you see him, remind him he owes me twenty bucks."

"What's with the balloon?" Mr. Five asked Sabrina as he lifted his little blue toboggan hat out of his eyes.

"It is King Puck's medicinal vessel!" Moth said indignantly.

"Smells like the N train coming back from Coney Island," Mr. Four grumbled.

Mr. Six spoke into his walkie-talkie. "Kenny, this is Mr. Six. I'm in train four-ninety-nine. Have there been any unusual sightings in the tunnels today?"

A voice on the other end grunted. "You mean like six little people driving a stolen subway car through the system?"

Mr. Six scowled and turned to the group. "Kenny's human.

We trust him—helped get him the job with the MTA—but he's a pain in the morning."

"Especially when he hasn't had his coffee," Mr. Four added.

"Kenny, I'm talking about fairies," Mr. Six said into the device. "You know, anyone report seeing a flying person with wings?"

There was silence on the other end, then Kenny responded, "Actually, there's a report of an incident at the Fifty-ninth Street station. Some woman claimed she saw an angel in the tunnel."

"Sounds like our fairy. When did it happen?" Bess asked.

Mr. Six repeated the question into his walkie-talkie.

"Five minutes ago," Kenny said.

"All right, pal, I'm on the six line coming up on Spring Street. I need to jump to the D line at Broadway-Lafayette."

"Thanks for the warning," Kenny said grumpily.

"Kenny, just do it!" Mr. Six shouted into the walkie-talkie. In no time, the train was racing into the Broadway-Lafayette station, where it jumped onto an intersecting track, forcing the car to make a hair-pin turn. Nearly everyone fell out of their seats and onto the floor.

"Cobweb is lucky you guys are going to catch him," Mr. Two said, as he helped everyone back into their seats. "If we caught him down here, we'd teach him a lesson he wouldn't soon forget. The tunnels belong to us."

"As if anyone else wants these filthy tunnels, half-breed," Moth sneered.

"You'll be singing a different tune when we strike it rich down here," Mr. Four said. "There's diamonds down here somewhere. I can smell 'em. All we have to do is find 'em."

Mr. Six raised his hand for quiet and held his walkie-talkie to his mouth. "Kenny, Six here again. I need you to switch us to the uptown A line at West Fourth Street."

The car was suddenly diverted again and whipped through the next tunnel so fast Sabrina was sure they would derail.

"I got him!" Mr. One shouted over the loudspeaker.

Everyone raced to join him at the front of the car. There, flying directly in front of the train, was Cobweb. He turned back to look at them, and Sabrina saw his face. It was angry and desperate. He flapped his wings even harder and zipped ahead.

"He's getting away, fool!" Moth cried. "Can't you make this hunk of junk go faster?"

"Oh, you don't talk about our train!" One shouted at her. "She's fast enough."

The train car sped through the tunnels, making turns at blistering speeds. It slammed through one station after another, blowing the newspapers and coffee cups out of the hands of waiting passengers. The whole time, Mr. Six was barking orders to Kenny on his walkie-talkie that sent the train jumping onto different lines. More than once they nearly collided with another train. If the constant near-crashes bothered the dwarfs, they didn't show it. In fact, they seemed almost bored by the whole experience.

Yet, no matter which way they steered the car, Cobweb was impossible to catch. He could easily switch to a different tunnel, or backtrack before the train car got a chance to maneuver.

Just as they were finally on top of the fairy, there was a loud thump on the roof of the car.

The dwarfs looked at one another with serious expressions.

"What?" Mr. Canis growled.

Mr. Four held a finger to his lips, urging him to be quiet. After a few seconds, there was another loud thump.

Mr. Five looked to the roof. "Uh-oh."

"What's *uh-oh* mean?" Granny asked.

"Yahoos," Five replied.

"Yahoos? What's a Yahoo?" Daphne asked.

"Dirty lunatics that keep invading our tunnels. Gulliver should never have brought them over here!" Mr. Six complained.

"You mean the Gulliver from *Gulliver's Travels*?" Sabrina asked.

"The same. He felt sorry for the little heathens and tried to civilize them by bringing them to the United States. They took over the Bowery and were happy enough playing in punk rock bands and working in coffee shops—you know, being worthless slackers—but now the neighborhood has been taken over by boutiques and health food stores. So they're in search of new turf and have been eyeing the tunnels all year."

There was another loud thump and one of the glass windows shattered. A thick, hairy hand reached into the car from outside.

Mr. Six swatted at it. "Dirty, stinking slackers. Go find another neighborhood to ruin. Haven't you ever heard of Brooklyn?"

Then the entire train started rocking back and forth. There was loud hooting and hollering, followed by more of the frightening pounding on the train.

"They're trying to derail us!" Mr. One shouted from his conductor seat. "If they keep rocking this train, we're going to jump right off the tracks and slam into the wall."

"That's bad, isn't it?" Daphne asked the little men. They all nodded.

"I've got an idea!" Mr. Two said. "But you're not going to like it. Let's slam on the brakes."

The rest of the men stared at him.

"You're right, we don't like it," Mr. Six said. "We'll just derail ourselves."

"That's the idea!" Mr. Two insisted. "We whip the car into South Ferry Station and then slam on the brakes."

"South Ferry is the end of the line, you imbecile!" Mr. Five shouted. "If we can't stop, we'll crash."

"Even if we can stop, the train will probably catch on fire," Mr. Three said. "The brakes can't handle the strain."

Another window shattered in the back of the train car.

Mr. Two shrugged. "It doesn't look like we have much choice. We can slam into the wall and get mangled in twisted metal or attempt to save ourselves but possibly die a fiery death."

"You fools cannot be serious," Mr. Canis said, rising to his feet. "Stop the train now, and I will get out and take care of these creatures myself."

"No can do, buddy," Mr. Six said. "We're in a tunnel, and these tracks are electrified. If you step on one you'd be an instant French fry."

"Grab onto something, people," Mr. One said over the loudspeaker. "Sorry we don't have any seat belts." The dwarfs scurried over to seats and hugged them tightly. The girls and their friends looked at one another in disbelief.

Mr. Six shouted into his walkie-talkie, "Kenny, we need you to clear the platform at South Ferry."

There was a groan on the other end of the line. "When?"

"Two minutes," Mr. Six replied.

"Two minutes?"

"Just do it, Kenny!"

Daphne wrapped her arms around Granny Relda. Even in all the chaos, Sabrina felt stung that the little girl would turn to their grandmother instead of her. Sabrina had been there for Daphne her whole life! Now it was like she didn't even exist.

"South Ferry is the final stop on this train!" Mr. One said over the loudspeaker. Then he raced out of the conductor's booth, climbed up onto one of the seats, and reached for a red cord on the wall. A sign above it read EMERGENCY BRAKE.

"You've got to be kidding!" Sabrina exclaimed. "This is how you guys stop your train?"

Mr. Hamstead wrapped his arms around Bess and pulled her to the floor.

"You gonna save my life again, cowboy?" she asked.

Hamstead nodded. "That's my job."

"I hope this hurts!" Mr. Six shouted to the Yahoos on the roof of the car just as Mr. One pulled the cord.

# 7

ALOUD, METALLIC SCREECH FILLED THE AIR. Sabrina jolted forward but managed to grab the center pole to steady herself. Still, the forward momentum of the car nearly pulled her arms out of their sockets. She hoped Daphne had been able to hold on, too, but she couldn't be certain in the dark.

The lights came back as they stopped just inside South Ferry Station, the last station, on the southern tip of Manhattan. Through the dingy windows she saw three odd men with thick arms and legs tumble off the top of the train. They fell with a horrible, bone-crunching sound, but as black smoke began to fill the car Sabrina wondered if the Yahoos were the lucky ones. This was her second fire in as many days, with flames and sparks shooting outside the train.

"Everyone off! This thing is going to go up in flames!" one of the dwarfs shouted. Sabrina did as she was told.

Mr. Two and Mr. Five helped everyone onto the platform, safely away from the fire. Even Puck's chrysalis floated out to join them. Moth grabbed its string, then whirled around to confront the group.

"You lost Cobweb, you fools," she cried.

"Shut your trap, Princess," Mr. Three said. "You're not so big that I can't take you."

Sabrina hugged her sister. "Are you OK?" She didn't wait for an answer. Instead, she started examining the little girl's arms and legs for broken bones or cuts.

"I'm fine," Daphne said, irritated. She struggled out of Sabrina's embrace.

"Good," Sabrina said, pretending not to be hurt. She looked around at the others. "We're all safe now. Everything is going to be OK. We're out of danger."

"Dwarfs go too far!" a voice shouted. Sabrina turned. One of the Yahoos, who only moments ago had been crumpled and broken on the floor, now stood tall on his feet. His friends joined him, forming a hairy band of modern-day cavemen in ironic T-shirts and cargo shorts.

"You don't want any of this, monkey-boy," Mr. Six threatened. "We may be small, but we can take all of you."

The Yahoos let loose high-pitched, sadistic laughter, just like the hyenas Sabrina had once seen at the Bronx Zoo. It sent shivers racing through her body.

"We take tunnels. Tunnels ours!" they cried.

Mr. One stepped forward. Much to Sabrina's amazement, he moved into a fighting stance identical to one Daphne had learned from her former teacher, Ms. White. It was an attack position from her Bad Apples self-defense class. He and his five brothers bowed to their opponents. Daphne ran to join them before Sabrina could stop her.

"Present your warrior faces!" Mr. One shouted.

At once, the six dwarfs and Daphne crinkled up their faces and roared like lions.

The Yahoos were twice as big as the dwarfs and, Sabrina guessed, ten times as strong. They beat on their chests like gorillas and stomped their feet.

"Come get some," taunted Mr. Two, and the groups attacked each other.

The dwarfs were fast and nimble. They leaped and flipped like kung fu masters, avoiding blows and delivering painful kicks to their opponents' faces. Daphne was in the midst of the fight, punching and kicking, though far less gracefully than the little men.

This was why Sabrina had to quit the family business. There was always some crazy danger rearing its head, and Daphne was never smart enough to run. Sabrina had to stop her.

Unfortunately, before she could act, Sabrina felt a tap on her shoulder. She spun around and found Cobweb hovering over her. She staggered in shock, but the fairy grabbed her arm to steady her.

"Was anyone injured?" he asked.

"N-no," Sabrina stammered, then mimicked her sister's stance.

"I'm not here to hurt you," the fairy promised. "I just want all of you to know I didn't hurt the king."

"Stop lying," Sabrina demanded. "Oberon's ghost told us you did it. If you don't come with us now, we're going to catch you and your Scarlet Hand buddies, too."

"My what?"

"Don't play dumb with me. We know you're involved with them. You left their mark on Oberon's body."

"Child, I have no idea what you are talking about," Cobweb said. "I'm not in any group, and I didn't kill Oberon!"

"Mustardseed says you'll get a chance to defend yourself. Just turn yourself in."

Moth spotted the dark fairy. "Murderer!" she cried. She reached into her pocket and took out a small flute, similar to the one Puck had used so many times. It summoned an army of tiny flying pixies he called his minions. Moth blew a few light notes of her own, then shoved the instrument back into her pocket.

"What did you just do, Moth?" Sabrina asked.

Suddenly, a wave of little lights hit Cobweb in the chest, slamming him into a nearby wall.

Granny grabbed the fairy girl by the arm and shook her. "Make them stop!"

Moth refused and pulled away.

Unable to defend himself, Cobweb ran up the station stairs with the pixies in pursuit. Moth raced after them.

"We have to stop this," Granny said to the group.

"Wait. Daphne!" Sabrina cried. Her sister and the dwarfs had successfully beaten the Yahoos back into the tunnels, and they were still celebrating. Sabrina raced over to Daphne, clamped her hand around her sister's arm, and dragged her up the station steps, with Granny and their friends following close behind. "Hey, let go of me!" Daphne shouted, but Sabrina ignored her. The little girl gave up and instead waved good-bye to the dwarfs, who were still cheering their victory. "I'll tell Mr. Seven you said hello!"

"Tell him I want my twenty bucks!" Mr. Two cried.

"Good luck, daughters of Veronica Grimm!" the little men shouted.

When the girls reached street level, Cobweb was gone. Moth paced nearby, screaming in rage. "We've lost him again!"

"I don't know who you're screaming at," Mr. Hamstead said angrily. "That psychotic stunt of yours was why he escaped."

"You blame me?" Moth shouted. "How dare you."

"Child!" Mr. Canis roared. "You have tested my patience long enough today!" He leaped forward, claws already drawn as if prepared to rip the fairy to shreds.

"Wolf!" Hamstead shouted, stepping between Moth and the old man. "Back away."

Canis eyed Hamstead for several moments.

"I can see you in there, mongrel," Hamstead said. "You come out and you'll get more of what the Three Little Pigs gave you the last time."

Something inside of Canis seethed but slunk back into the old man. Most of his wolflike features faded away, as well.

Hamstead turned and addressed everyone. "We need to re-group here, folks. We're trying to catch Cobweb. Not kill him." He looked at Moth. "And we shouldn't be fighting amongst our-selves. If you can't work as part of a team, you should go back to the hotel. 'Cause to be honest, you're in the way."

Moth shot him a sour look then turned away. She muttered something under her breath.

Bess gave Hamstead an admiring look and a squeeze on the arm. He turned bright pink.

"Look, Cobweb left footprints in the snow," Daphne said, fi-nally pulling free of her sister.

"Daphne Grimm! Well done!" Mr. Hamstead said. "If we fol-low these prints, they'll lead us right to him."

Everyone nodded, even Moth, and they set off to follow the tracks. As they walked, Sabrina tried to engage her sister.

"It was stupid of you to get into that fight," she said.

"You're stupid," Daphne said.

"You could have been hurt. Why would you take such a risk?"

"I'm going to have to take bigger risks now that I'm on my own," Daphne replied.

Sabrina stopped in her tracks, watching as her sister hurried to catch up with Mr. Canis, who was leading their group.

Granny joined Sabrina and gave her a sad smile. "This is her choice, *liebling*."

"So I should just let her get killed?"

Granny shook her head. "As long as I'm around, I won't let that happen."

The footprints led to Battery Park. In warmer weather, the place would be filled with tourists waiting for boats to ferry them over to the Statue of Liberty and Ellis Island. Now it was almost empty. Even the Staten Island Ferry, a commuter boat that took people to the city's remote island borough, was deserted, though one set of footprints in the snow led right to its main terminal. Cobweb was clearly planning to take the next ferry. Sabrina helped her grandmother through the snow and into the waiting area. There, the group drew stares from the terminal staff. Sabrina realized that most were gazing at Mr. Canis—who still had fangs and a tail.

"Look, there's Cobweb!" Moth shouted. Sabrina turned in the direction the fairy pointed, only to see a boat pulling away from the dock. Cobweb sat on the railing looking back at them. His face was grim and cold.

"I'll get him!" Moth said as her fairy wings popped out of her back.

Granny snatched her arm. "We'll wait for the next boat."

Moth reluctantly retracted her wings.

"By the time we get to Staten Island, Cobweb will be long gone," Daphne said.

"You have bigger problems than that," a rough voice said from behind them. Sabrina turned around and saw half a dozen men with copper skin and jet black hair coming toward them. Their leader had dark eyes as fierce as any she had ever seen. "You know as well as I do that fairy folk are not welcome on docks controlled by Sinbad the Sailor."

Sabrina instinctively stepped between her sister and the stranger. She'd read parts of *One Thousand and One Nights* recently while researching jinni in hopes one might help her rescue her parents. The story of Sinbad was fresh in her memory. He'd set sail on seven voyages and seen some fairly amazing things, including ogres, jinni, and fish disguised as massive islands. He'd killed hordes of monsters, too, but each voyage nearly killed him. She didn't remember him as a villain—maybe a little dim, but more of a good-hearted adventurer. Still, in the time she had spent in Ferryport Landing she knew better than to assume the good guys were still good. More than a few had switched sides. "Since when?" Moth said angrily to the sailor. "You can't deny a princess of the royal court!"

The sailor's men pulled nasty-looking daggers out of their coats.

Sinbad smiled. "I can deny you anything I choose. Oberon forced us to pay his lousy taxes for centuries, but he's dead now. I'm not about to let one just like him come in here and take our hard-earned money again."

"We're not fairies," Daphne said. "We're detectives, and we're trying to find the person who killed Oberon."

Sinbad cocked an eyebrow and studied Daphne closely. "It can't be! Can it? Am I in the presence of Veronica Grimm's child?"

"Children," Sabrina said, stepping forward.

The men put their daggers away.

"I am honored to meet you," Sinbad said. "It was a dark day in my heart when your mother vanished."

"Please, bore us with another story of the great and beautiful Veronica Grimm," Moth grumbled.

"What brings you here?" Sinbad asked, ignoring Moth.

"The fairy suspected of killing King Oberon is on the boat that just left," Granny Relda said. "We need to get on the next one if we have any chance of catching him."

Sinbad looked at his men, then back at the group. "I may be able to be of some assistance," he said, and led everyone to the next docking station. He took out a key, unlocked a huge door, and slid it open. Behind it was a second ferryboat.

"You've got your own boat?" Hamstead asked.

"Of course! I am the harbormaster," Sinbad said proudly, helping them board. He then started the boat's engine as his men untied its mooring lines from the dock. In no time, they were cruising away from Manhattan in pursuit of Cobweb.

"Chasing a murderer . . . is this not dangerous work for such young girls?" Sinbad asked.

"We're Grimms and this is what we do," Daphne said.

Sinbad laughed. "Your mother used to say the same thing whenever I had to help her out of one of her many close calls. Not that I minded. I have to admit, I was quite taken with her."

"You had a crush on our mother?" Daphne asked.

"Crush? I was head over heels! Veronica was quite a woman, and I've known a great many in my day. She was brilliant and strong, if a bit stubborn."

"Sounds like someone I know," Granny said, flashing Sabrina a smile.

"I asked her to run away with me nearly a thousand times, but she always rebuffed me. She said she only had eyes for your father. The fates were smiling on him the day he met her."

Sabrina was livid. Hearing the sailor talk about her mother this way was infuriating. Sinbad noticed and smiled.

"Little one, allow a man to dream. Your mother never took my advances seriously. Most of the time she was too busy with her plans to fix our community to even notice I was flirting."

One of Sinbad's crew raced to the bridge. He looked nervous and sweaty. "My lord, we have a problem."

"What is it?"

"Pirates!"

"Again?" Sinbad scowled. "This is the third time this week they have meddled in my affairs! Very well, if they are looking for a fight, a fight they shall get. Alert the crew!"

His man smiled and raced off to tell his colleagues.

"Pirates? What pirates?" Sabrina cried as she scanned the horizon. Sinbad didn't answer. Instead, he rushed out onto the deck. The Grimms and their friends followed to find the entire crew standing on one side of the boat peering through binoculars.

Sabrina snatched a pair for herself and scanned the harbor. Sailing near the Statue of Liberty was a boat with a black flag waving in the wind. The flag had a smiling skull and crossbones on it. She watched a torch's flame fluttering on the other deck, then heard an enormous explosion. A moment later something big crashed into the water not far from the ferry.

"How dare they! I am Sinbad, master of the sea! Steer into their path and see how brave they are with our cutlasses at their throats," he commanded. His men cheered and raced to their stations. A moment later the ferry made an abrupt turn and headed straight for the approaching pirates.

"What are you doing?" Mr. Canis demanded. "We're after a killer. We have no interest in your petty turf war!"

"You have nothing to fear, my friend, praise be. I am Sinbad, and I have faced these foul vermin before. Though maybe we should arm you. Men, hand out some steel!"

The crew shoved large swords into everyone's hands.

"What are we supposed to do with these?" Sabrina asked, alarmed.

"They're quite useful for killing pirates," Sinbad said as he hurried back to the bridge.

"I don't think I'm allowed to kill pirates!" Daphne called after him. She looked up at Granny Relda. "Am I?"

The old woman shook her head, collected the children's swords, and leaned them in a corner.

Another member of the crew rushed toward them with a dagger between his teeth and his arms full of life jackets. He passed them out to Sabrina and the others.

"What do we need these for?" Hamstead asked as there was another loud splash off the side of the boat.

"In case we have to jump overboard," the man replied.

"Why would we have to jump overboard?"

"If the boat is about to blow up," the sailor said matter-of-factly.

Hamstead cringed and turned to Sabrina. "Pigs don't swim," he whispered nervously.

There was an enormous crash, and the cabin wall they were standing next to exploded, sending wood and glass everywhere. Sabrina tumbled to the floor.

"We've taken a hit!" Sinbad shouted. "It's time to show those devils what kind of men they're dealing with! Let's do this old school, shall we?"

The crew roared in approval. One of men rushed to a panel on the wall. Inside was a red button, which he pounded hard with his fist. Suddenly, the top of the ferry flew off and crashed into the water. Two holes opened up in the deck and long wooden poles soared skyward. When both were extended to their fullest height, huge sails unfurled from the tops. The crew quickly went about tying them into position. The cold winter wind heaved against the boat, and Sabrina felt it pick up speed.

Sinbad's voice rose above the din. "Stand clear for artillery load in."

More slots opened along both sides of the boat and heavy black cannons were pushed into place, each with a pyramid of cannon-balls stacked nearby. Several of the men rolled huge wooden kegs, one for each cannon. The kegs had the words GUNPOWDER and DANGER printed on the sides.

"We have to get off this thing!" Sabrina cried. She grabbed her sister and grandmother and raced to the edge of the boat, looking back to make sure Puck's cocoon and the rest of her group were following. She was prepared to jump overboard, but when she peered into the black water below Sabrina realized how very cold it would be—the freezing temperature would mean instant death.

They were trapped onboard, with a captain and crew who were laughing in the face of danger. When another cannonball landed just short of the boat and splashed into the water, they booed as if disappointed in their attackers' poor aim.

"Ladies, would you like to set off the return volley?" Sinbad asked, suddenly appearing before them, holding a flaming torch.

Sabrina looked at the elated smile on the man's face. He might have been good to her mother, but it seemed he couldn't care less if Veronica's daughters were blown to bits. Sabrina thought about how she so often found herself in these situations, the kind where people got hurt, and she wasn't going to take it anymore. Without even thinking it through, she lunged forward, snatched the sword from Sinbad's belt, and leveled it at his head.

"Take us back to the dock," she said calmly.

"You look so much like your mother right now," Sinbad said, shifting his eyes back and forth from her face to the sword poking at his throat.

"I've had enough craziness. Turn the boat around and take us back to the dock. You're not going to get us killed, especially before I get to retire," she said.

"Child, we are in the middle of a fight. If we turn this boat, the pirates will fire on our port side and we'll surely go down," Sinbad argued.

"Sabrina, give him back the sword," Granny Relda demanded.

"NO! This is exactly what I'm talking about when I say I don't want to be a Grimm. Look at these maniacs. They're having fun. And you know why? Because they can't die unless someone tries really hard to kill them. This is just a stupid game to them. Well, I can die, Granny, and so can you and Daphne. So, Sinbad here is going to turn this boat around right now."

Daphne rushed to Sabrina's side and snatched the sword away.

"You're being a jerkazoid!" she shouted.

"I'm trying to protect us. I'm trying to save us all!" Sabrina cried.

"So is he," Daphne said, pointing at Sinbad. "Those pirates fired on us first."

She handed Sinbad back his weapon.

"You're a spirited girl," Sinbad said to Sabrina. "If a bit odd smelling."

Before Sabrina could argue with her sister, she heard a horn blast and watched as the men adjusted the sail riggings, tying them down tight. The sails trapped the wind, and again the ferry picked up speed. Sabrina could hardly believe the power of the blustery winter air; the boat was cutting through the waves as if propelled by rockets.

Sinbad peered through his binoculars again. "We're close enough to see the faces of the mongrels now." He handed the binoculars to Hamstead, who took a peek as well.

"Uh, those aren't pirates," Hamstead said. "They're wearing suits and ties."

Sabrina snatched the binoculars out of his hand and saw that Hamstead was right. The approaching boat wasn't a pirate ship at all but a yacht. Its passengers seemed to be sipping cocktails between cannon shots.

"Is this a joke?" Sabrina said, yanking on Sinbad's sleeve.

"What do you mean?" the roguish sailor said.

"Those aren't pirates. They look like they work on Wall Street."

"I believe they call themselves corporate raiders," Bess said.

The bridge above exploded as a cannonball smacked into it, turning it to splinters. The two men steering the boat jumped to safety at the last second.

Sinbad shouted to his men. "They're coming alongside! Let's give them a good fight, praise be."

The men cheered, and when the "pirate" boat was close enough, Sinbad leaped over the gap, landed onboard the yacht, and started fighting a man wearing a three-piece suit. Their blades slashed the air, the tips each coming within a whisper of the other. Several of the invaders, who were also very well dressed, some holding glasses of brandy, mimicked Sinbad's bravery and jumped from the yacht onto the ferryboat. The crew charged them, and a savage battle erupted around the Grimms and their friends. Everywhere Sabrina looked, she saw sparks shooting from clanging blades.

Mr. Canis leaped into action. He led Sabrina, Daphne, Granny, and Moth through the melee, doing his best to avoid getting slashed himself. Puck's chrysalis floated close behind, missing several near-punctures. Hamstead and Bess were in tow, and together they all charged down a flight of steps leading into the boat's hold. Unfortunately, they were followed by a huge man with a wicked scar running from the tip of his right eye to the edge of his lip. He was dressed as sharply as the other pirates, with golden cuff links and a fancy tie pin, but his clothing didn't lend him the same charm as his colleagues. He roared at the family. Canis turned and roared back. The pirate stood there for a moment, as if trying to understand who or what Canis was, then ran back up the steps.

"They'll follow us down here soon enough," Mr. Canis said. "Stay down here and hide. I'll see if I can help Sinbad."

"Me, too," Hamstead added.

"Ernest, be careful," Bess said, squeezing his hand.

In a flash, the two men were gone.

"You heard him, girls," Granny said. "Find a place to hide."

They searched the ship for a nook to scurry into, but there wasn't enough time. A mob of pirates stampeded down the steps and cornered them.

"Hostages!" one of them exclaimed as he licked his blade. "The boss will be pleased."

The rest laughed.

"Take 'em to Silver," someone shouted. Daphne kicked one of the men in the shin, and he fell to the floor in pain. Granny smacked another with her heavy handbag and split his lip. Bess and Moth threw punches. Sabrina was grabbed around the neck, but she instinctively jammed her elbow deep into her attacker's belly. The rogue bent over and dropped his sword. Sabrina snatched it off the floor and smacked him on the behind with the flat of the blade. Moth took a life preserver off the wall and brought it crashing down on his head, and he fell to the floor unconscious.

Much to Sabrina's surprise, the pirates broke off their attack and rushed up the steps.

"Where are they going?" Sabrina wondered.

"They know not to mess with us," Daphne crowed.

"We make a pretty good team, don't we, ladies?" Bess said.

But there was no time to celebrate. The pirates returned with reinforcements. They grabbed Sabrina, Daphne, and Moth and hauled the girls up onto the deck. A moment later the pirates hoisted them over the side of the ship, where they landed unceremoniously on the deck of the yacht. Puck's cocoon, never far from Sabrina, floated after them. Seconds later, the pirates gave up their assault on the ferry and returned to their own boat. With its powerful engine it zipped away, leaving Sinbad, his crew, Granny Relda, Canis, Hamstead, and Bess watching from the ferry.

"The harbor belongs to Silver!" one of the pirates bellowed

toward the ferry, causing all the rogues to cheer and raise their swords in the air. Many of them broke into song and danced little jigs. The girls didn't get to see much of this gloating. They were dragged roughly down a flight of steps toward the belly of the yacht.

"Get your hands off me, filth," Moth demanded. "I am a princess of the royal court."

"Nice to meet you, Princess," one of the pirates said in a thick English accent. "Now get yourself through that door."

"And if I don't?" she said.

"Then you're going to miss the party." He opened the door, and Sabrina gawked at what she saw. There were a dozen more well-dressed men and women on a small dance floor in the center of the room. A disc jockey was playing records, and a glittery disco ball threw sparkling light around the room. A banner reading HAPPY HOLIDAYS TO EVERYONE AT SILVER AND HAWKINS! hung over everything.

"What is this?" Sabrina asked.

"It's our firm's Christmas party," the pirate replied.

"What?" the girls said in unison.

A tall, gray-haired man hobbled over to them. He had a parrot on his shoulder and walked with a cane. Like the others, he was impeccably dressed. He set down his cocktail and extended his hand to the captives.

"So good of you to join us. I'm John Silver," he said.

Sabrina and the others said nothing.

"As in Long John Silver," he continued.

Still, the girls were silent.

"As in *Treasure Island*, documented by Robert Louis Stevenson," Silver said hopefully.

"I've seen the movie," Daphne said. "You're not very nice."

"Everyone has seen that lousy movie. Doesn't anyone read anymore?" the pirate asked with a scowl. "The book really captures more of my complexities."

The pirates roared with laughter.

"Aren't you supposed to have a peg leg?" the little girl asked.

Silver lifted his pant cuff to reveal a prosthetic leg. "It's the twenty-first century, dearie. This is the latest model."

"You'll regret this, pirate," Moth seethed.

The crowd booed.

"*Pirate* is such an ugly word," Silver explained. "Pirates are criminals. We're bankers. We've traded in doubloons and treasure for stocks and bonds."

The parrot squawked. "Buy low, sell high!"

"I've never heard of bankers attacking boats full of children and old ladies," Sabrina said.

"Yes, most unfortunate. I hate that you got caught up in our little financial dispute. Controlling the ports is a lucrative business, especially now that Oberon isn't around to stop us. Sinbad and his dirty friends stand in the way of a substantial windfall."

"Aren't you worried that someone is going to notice a yacht firing cannons at the Staten Island Ferry?" Sabrina said.

"Kid, they may call New York the city that never sleeps, but they should call it the city that never notices. We could sail up the East River and attack the mayor's mansion, and I doubt it would even make the papers."

"Listen, whatever your problem is with Sinbad, it has nothing to do with us. Why don't you drop us off at the dock, and we'll let you get back to your fun," Sabrina said.

The crowd erupted into laughter.

"I'm afraid that's not possible," Silver said. "You see, you're not exactly guests—you're hostages."

"What does *hostages* mean?" Daphne asked, finally turning to Sabrina for help.

"It means he's going to trade us for money," Sabrina said, then turned back to Silver. "You won't get anything out of Sinbad. We just met him half an hour ago."

"Don't flatter yourself, human. Clearly he plans to extort the queen for my release," Moth said.

"Not quite, fairy," Silver said. "The children of Veronica Grimm are invaluable. Someone will pay handsomely for them. Friends, we're going to get a payday to rival our holiday bonuses!"

The pirates cheered.

"Now, the rules of the sea say we treat our prisoners with civility, so help yourselves to the buffet. The DJ will be playing for another half hour, and then we're going to do some karaoke. Relax and try to have some fun, but don't even think about singing 'Love Shack.' That's my song."

"Silver!" Moth cried. "You will never get away with this."

"I never get tired of hearing people say that to me," the pirate said, joining the others in a raucous laugh.

Moth snarled and spit in the pirate's face. Silver calmly reached into his pocket and pulled out a handkerchief to clean himself off. Then he took a long, curved knife from the cheese table and aimed the point at Moth's face.

"You have a nasty mouth," Silver said. "Though I suppose I could fix that by cutting your tongue out."

The crowd roared its approval.

Suddenly, there was a bright flicker at one of the port windows. Sabrina looked out but didn't see anything. Maybe all the stress was getting to her.

"Leave her alone," Daphne pleaded. "She won't be any more trouble."

"Shut your yap, child!" Silver shouted as he dropped his cane and grabbed Daphne by the throat. "I'd hate to lose you, too, but I'm sure one Grimm girl would be nearly as valuable as two."

"Take your hands off her," Sabrina yelled as she rushed at the rogue. He swung his knife away from Moth and toward her, stopping a fraction of an inch away from her throat.

"Keep it up, girlie, and you'll be able to breathe out of your neck," he said.

"Your stock is falling!" the parrot squawked.

Just then, the door into the hold flew off its hinges. A dark figure stepped into the room. It was Cobweb.

"Come, girls. We're leaving," he announced, then opened his mouth and shot a stream of fire at the pirates. They fled in every direction, giving the girls enough time to rush back up to the deck of the yacht. Puck's cocoon followed closely behind.

"Cobweb just saved us!" Daphne said. "If he's guilty, why would he do that?"

Sabrina shrugged. "Let's worry about getting off this boat. He might come back up here and change his mind."

The girls searched the ship, but there was no lifeboat to be found; worse, the pirates were already charging up onto the deck. Long John Silver hobbled up from below, followed by a dozen angry men with daggers. Two of them were dragging Cobweb.

"You know, there's one thing I've learned during my time on Wall Street—you have to weigh the value of investments," Silver bellowed as he came toward the girls, who were now trapped against the ship's railing. "Take you Grimms, for instance. The both of you could be worth your weight in gold—but then again, it may be just as valuable to me to watch you and your fairy friends walk the plank."

"Bad investment!" the parrot shrieked. "Sell! Sell! Sell!"

One of Silver's men rushed up from below with a long plank of wood. He set it on the edge of the yacht while another pirate nailed it into place. Once it was secure, Silver pulled the cheese knife out of his belt and forced Sabrina to climb up onto the plank.

"Don't hurt my sister!" Daphne yelled. She tried to grab at Sabrina's shirt to pull her back on deck, but one of the pirates yanked the little girl away.

"Let them go, Silver," Cobweb demanded, but he got a punch in the belly for his efforts.

"Wait your turn," Silver snarled.

Sabrina walked to the edge of the plank and looked down at the icy water. *This is the second time I've been on one of these things*, she remembered. Puck had forced her to walk a plank above their neighbor's pool the first time they met. He had used his pixies to get her up on the diving board.

"Excuse me," Sabrina said suddenly. "Don't I get a last request?"

Silver smiled. "Indeed. Name it."

"I'd like my good friend Moth to play us a song on her flute. Something happy before we die."

"You are as dumb as a cow!" Moth cried. "You get one last wish, and you want a song?"

Sabrina looked at Daphne. "Yes, a song like the one Puck used to play for us. One so sad it stings."

Daphne's eyes grew wide with understanding. "Yes, Moth, play a song on your flute."

Cobweb cocked his eyebrows. "Princess, might I suggest a particular song? I've always loved 'Flight of the Pixies.'"

Moth rolled her eyes and took her wooden flute out of the folds of her dress. Sabrina was sure the little fairy was too thick to understand what they wanted her to do, but she lifted the instrument to her mouth and blew a few short notes. When she was done, nothing happened.

"Uh, wasn't there a second verse?" Sabrina said.

"No, there isn't a second verse," Moth snapped.

"Then play it again!" Sabrina cried.

"I thought she only got one last request!" Moth lifted the flute again and blew the same notes.

"All right, that's enough," Silver said.

"But wait, you filthy crab, what about your last request?" Moth asked.

"Why would I need a last request?" Silver said.

"Because you're under attack," the little fairy girl replied. A split second later, the entire yacht was enveloped in an enormous swarm of lights. They swirled around the pirates, who swatted at them to little effect. The pixies were everywhere, and they were stinging with all their might. Silver swung his dagger wildly as little dots of blood appeared on his face, while his men raced into the belly of the boat, hoping to escape the swarm. When he realized his men were gone, Silver hobbled quickly after them.

The wave of pixies became one giant mass that hovered next to Moth, awaiting her orders. The little princess stepped over to Cobweb, who had fallen on the deck in the chaos and was now trying to catch his breath.

"Now I will deal with you," Moth said.

"Moth, no!" Sabrina said. She moved to stop the fairy, but the pixies surrounded her. One stung her neck, a warning of the thousands more she would receive if she tried to stop Moth.

"I'm innocent," Cobweb said as he got to his feet. "I would never hurt Oberon. I supported his efforts to rebuild the kingdom. I worked closely with him to make his vision a reality."

"What are you talking about?" Sabrina asked.

"Oberon wanted to build a clinic, and a school for our children. He was going to establish a permanent home for us. He had plans, and they were already underway. The taxes we got from the citizens were going to be used to make everyone's lives better. He was preparing to announce the opening of a shelter for homeless Everafters. He had so many ideas, many he got after conversations with Veronica."

Sabrina was stunned. She'd despised Oberon from the moment she met him, even secretly feeling that his death was justified, especially after hearing about his goons extorting money from the citizens and bullying everyone into obedience. But now, Cobweb was describing a completely different person—or at least, a person Oberon was trying to be. It didn't make sense that Cobweb would kill a person he respected so much. Sabrina turned to her sister, who looked just as amazed, and then to Moth. The little fairy's jaw was set and her eyes were narrowed. It was clear she was not moved by Cobweb's story. In fact, she had murder in her eyes.

"Take him!" Moth shouted, and the pixies swarmed after the dark fairy—but Cobweb's wings were out and he was aloft faster than Sabrina would have thought possible. Within seconds he was out of the pixies' reach and rising higher and higher.

"Use the cannon," Moth instructed, and the swarm darted to the big gun, working together to load a ball inside and fill it with gunpowder.

"Moth, don't!" Daphne cried. "This isn't how you do things."

The fairy ignored her. She opened her mouth and a stream of fire shot out, igniting the cannon's wick. There was an earth-shaking roar, and the deck buckled beneath them. Sabrina watched a black missile speed into the air and slam into Cobweb's back. The fairy fell from the sky and plunged into the water.

"No!" Sabrina cried. She found a life preserver and tossed it overboard, even though she knew it was pointless. Even an Everafter couldn't survive that kind of injury. "You killed him!"

Moth shrugged. "Your job was to find Oberon's killer. Congratulations. You are no longer needed. Find your grandmother and your friends and go back to the mud hole you call home."

The pixies swarmed around Puck's chrysalis, latching onto it. Moth unfurled her wings and, together with the pixies, lifted Puck into the air, taking the cocoon up and away.

In the distant water, Sabrina spotted flashing blue lights heading in their direction. "This is the Coast Guard," a booming voice called out. "Lower your weapons and prepare to be boarded."

# 8

S ABRINA AND DAPHNE WERE TAKEN INTO custody by social services. A friendly man named Mr. Glassman, who insisted they call him Peter, spent several hours trying to track down Granny Relda. By the time she arrived to claim the girls, it was nearly two in the morning and friendly Peter had lost his patience.

"These children were found on a yacht in the middle of New York Harbor, Mrs. Grimm," Peter said sternly.

Granny smiled uncomfortably and shifted in her seat. "This has all been a misunderstanding. The girls and I were separated, and—"

"So you were supposed to be on the yacht, too?"

"Why, no—"

"We told you what happened. We were kidnapped," Daphne said.

"Young lady, the police have searched the boat. There was no one on it. In fact, the owner, a Mr. John Silver, is considering pressing charges against you for stealing it from the marina."

"Forgetful dust," Daphne grumbled. When the Coast Guard boarded the yacht, the pirates had used the magical memory eraser to make a getaway.

Sabrina kicked her sister under the table and shook her head. The less crazy their story sounded, the better off they would be.

The social worker took a deep breath. "Yes, the forgetful dust. Children, I was your age once. I loved magical stories about fairies and pirates. They're fun, but you need to learn the difference between reality and fantasy."

"Well, I think the girls learned their lesson," Granny said as she moved to stand. "I'm sure you have other things to worry about. I'll take the girls and get out of your hair."

"Mrs. Grimm, I'm afraid that's impossible," Peter said. "We need to evaluate your caretaking skills. We can't just let you take the girls if they are going to find themselves in danger again."

"How long will this evaluation take?" Granny asked.

"A few weeks at least."

"A few weeks!" the girls cried.

Daphne nudged Granny. "Throw some forgetful dust on him."

Peter rolled his eyes. "In the meantime, the state will retain custody of the girls," he continued.

"But who's going to take care of them?" Granny Relda asked anxiously.

There was a knock on the office door. Standing on the threshold was a gaunt woman with a face Sabrina would never forget. She had thin lips, a hooked nose, and dull gray hair.

"Hello, Ms. Smirt," Peter said. "Please come in."

The orphanage was exactly as Sabrina remembered. The floors were still filthy, the sheets still moth-eaten, and the kids still miserable. Much like Ms. Smirt herself, it was nasty, ancient, and drained of color.

Smirt led them through the main sleeping room, which was little more than a hallway with two rows of tightly packed cots, each containing a sleeping child. Sabrina and Daphne were assigned the last two, then forced to change into what Smirt called "orphanage attire," bright orange jumpsuits that reminded Sabrina of prison uniforms. When the girls were changed, Ms. Smirt hurried them to her office.

Smirt eyed the girls with contempt. "Imagine what a surprise it is to see my two favorite orphans, Sally and Denise."

"First, we're not orphans," Sabrina corrected. "Second, I'm Sabrina and this is Daphne."

"Yes, the Grimm sisters, the bane of my existence," the woman replied.

"Let's cut to the chase," Daphne said. "You're going to send us to live with some nutcase and we're going to escape like we always do. Why not just give us back to our grandmother? At least then we're out of your hair."

Sabrina was stunned by her sister's bold speech. It sounded like something she would have said herself.

Smirt smiled, a rare and frightening sight. "Well, if you would kindly explain your plan to the city, I'm all for it. Unfortunately, I'm required by law to keep trying to place you in a decent home, no matter how pointless that may be."

She opened a drawer in her desk, took out some forms, and scribbled notes. Sabrina could read them upside down. Smirt described them as "incorrigible troublemakers" and underlined her assessment after adding several exclamation points at the end.

"Luckily for me," the caseworker announced, "I've already found you a foster home that is willing to take you."

"We don't want to go to a foster home. Our grandmother is going to take us back as soon as she can," Daphne said.

"That is highly unlikely. The state doesn't make a habit of letting people take care of children who encourage them to risk their lives on the high seas. Maybe someday . . . when I'm in charge," Smirt said wistfully. "But for now you're going to live with Mr. Greeley."

Their caseworker snatched a folder off a stack of books and opened it. Sabrina noticed the title of the book on top. It was called *The Purpose-Driven Life*.

"Mr. David Greeley is currently in prison, but he's getting out tomorrow and will pick you up as soon as he's done meeting with his parole officer," Smirt said.

"Prison! What was he in prison for?" Sabrina asked.

"Hmmm, let me see. Oh, here it is. Murder," the caseworker said.

"Murder?" the girls cried, nearly jumping out of their chairs.

"Yes, he murdered someone—no, I'm wrong. That was someone else," Ms. Smirt said.

Relieved, Sabrina eased back in her seat.

"No, Mr. Greeley murdered several people, seven to be exact. Says here he beat them to death with a crowbar," Smirt said.

"You're going to send us to live with a serial killer?" Sabrina asked.

"No, I'm sending you to live with a former serial killer. Mr. Greeley is rehabilitated. Now, off to bed with you. Newbies have to fix breakfast for everyone, so you better get some sleep."

Smirt shoved the girls down the hall and back into the sleeping area. They found their beds at the end of the rows of snoring children, and crawled underneath the scratchy blankets. Before Ms. Smirt left, she cuffed one of each girl's hands to her bed.

Sabrina's cot was next to a window with a baseball-sized hole in it. The winter wind blew directly onto her feet, so she tucked herself into a ball for warmth.

"Well, I suppose you're happy now," Daphne said when Smirt scurried back to her office.

"Happy? Why would I be happy about this?"

"It's what you wanted, right? To get away from Granny, the

Everafters, and Ferryport Landing? Now you can pretend none of it ever happened."

"Daphne, I—"

"You have fought her since she came into our lives. You've complained and disobeyed and been a real—"

"Jerkazoid?"

"Yes!" the little girl cried. "And don't use my word."

"Daphne, I've only tried to protect us, all of us. Can't you see what has been happening since we moved in with Granny? I accidentally killed a giant. I nearly got Mr. Canis killed when the school exploded—and look what's happening to him now. Puck had his wings torn off trying to protect me, and now Cobweb is dead, too. Everywhere we go there's real danger. Sometimes it feels like we're cursed."

"That's crazy talk," the little girl whispered.

"I don't want to be a fairy-tale detective. Neither did Dad. He saw what I see, and when he got the opportunity to walk away, he took it. We should, too. I don't want you to get killed or fall under some twisted nutcase's magical spell. I want us to get out now, while we still can. Look at Mom. She was caught up in it, too. This whole time I always assumed our parents were kidnapped because of something Dad had done, but maybe it was Mom."

"Mom was trying to help people," Daphne said. "We're Grimms. That's what we do. We help people."

"Daphne, I—"

"No. I'm not listening to you anymore. This is what I want to do, and you can't change my mind. I'm getting out of here, finding Granny, and going back to Ferryport Landing. You can come with me if you want, but I'm going with or without you!"

Daphne turned her back on Sabrina and grew very still, signaling that this conversation was officially over. Sabrina guessed she had gone too far this time. In the past she had been a jerkazoid, she couldn't deny it, but this time she was truly thinking of others more than herself. Why did she have to make decisions like this, anyway? Worrying about how to keep everyone alive wasn't something she should have to do. She wasn't even twelve years old.

With her free hand, she reached for her coat at the end of her bed, searched its pockets, and found her mom's wallet. She opened it up and found the picture she loved. She stared into her mother's face, suddenly unsure of who Veronica Grimm really was. Why had Veronica chosen this life when she didn't have to? Why wouldn't anyone, given the choice, just walk away?

Smirt woke them early, unlocking their handcuffs and dragging them to the orphanage's kitchen, where they were put to work on breakfast, a disturbing combination of powdered eggs, leftovers, and milk with a questionable expiration date. A hulking man, who wore hairnets on both his head and beard, instructed them to add to the mix whatever he handed them out of the fridge. Several full catfish went into the pot—heads, bones, eyes, and all. Next, a bottle of barbecue sauce, a greasy package of bologna, and some mushrooms that might have been picked out of the orphanage's basement.

When all the ingredients were added, the girls had to stir the concoction with a huge wooden spoon, nearly as big as an oar. Every couple of seconds, a bubble would rise to the surface and pop, emitting a hot plume of steam that scalded their hands. The whole ordeal was pure misery for Sabrina, but it was made much worse by Daphne's silence. She tried to talk to her sister several times, but the girl's cold shoulder rivaled the winter storm outside. Deep down, Sabrina wished Daphne would call her "snot" or "jerkazoid," but the little girl refused to acknowledge her even enough to insult her.

When "breakfast" was ready, the girls were required to serve it to all the half-asleep children who staggered through the meal line. There were many faces Sabrina recognized, kids who would probably be in the orphanage until they were adults. None of them seemed to notice that the Grimm sisters had returned, except for Harold Dink. Harold was a freckle-faced kid with a skin condition that resembled mange; many patches of his bright red hair were missing. When he got to the counter he sneered, pointed, and laughed. "Hey, everybody! Look! The Sisters Ugly are right back where they started."

"You know, Harold, you should really be nice to the people who are serving you breakfast. You never know what might accidentally fall into your eggs," Daphne said.

"You don't have the guts, geek."

Even though Daphne wasn't speaking to her, Sabrina instinctively came to her defense. "Hey, Harold! Why don't you go steal some more money out of Smirt's office, then pretend you found it for her? How did that turn out the last time? Didn't she send you to live in a petting zoo?"

The kids in line roared with laughter. Harold slammed down his tray and stomped away.

Sabrina and Daphne were the last ones allowed to eat, though neither had much of an appetite for what was left at the bottom of the pot. Instead, they grabbed a couple of slices of stale bread and found a seat in the back of the cafeteria. Sabrina took a bite and cringed. The bread was as tough as cardboard.

"I suppose we're going to meet Greeley today," she said. But despite their united assault on Harold, Daphne didn't respond. Defeated, Sabrina went back to her bread and hoped she wouldn't lose a tooth.

David Greeley was a lanky guy with stringy muscles and thin chicken legs. His face could have used a shave two weeks earlier. A crooked smile matched his crooked teeth. His forearms were covered in sloppy tattoos, many of which looked as if they had been done while riding a horse.

"Yo!" he said when he met them on the front steps of the orphanage.

"Say hello to your new daddy," Ms. Smirt said as she reached down and gave each of the girls one of her trademark pinches on the shoulder.

Sabrina nodded at their new foster father, but Daphne said nothing.

"Good, they're quiet. Nothing worse than a couple of yapping kids," the man said. "I had a neighbor whose dog made a lot of noise. He ain't got no yapping dog anymore, if you know what I mean." Greeley made a gesture as if he were cocking a shotgun.

Daphne narrowed her eyes and looked as if she was preparing to kick the man in the shins. Sabrina stopped her with a warning hand on the shoulder.

Greeley bent over and rubbed the girls' heads as if they were beagles. "Let's get some things straight, girls. I'm in charge. I don't take no guff, and I don't give no guff."

"What does *guff* mean?" Daphne asked.

Sabrina shrugged.

"It means lip, sass, back talk, disrespect," Greeley answered. "I'm your father now, and as your old man I expect you to stay in line. You do what I say without question, and things will go smoothly. You don't do what I say, then we're going to have problems. There's only one way to do things—my way or the highway."

"So, just to be clear, you want us to do what you tell us to do," Sabrina said, though she knew the sarcasm was lost on Greeley. He nodded and smiled. Smirt, on the other hand, gave her another pinch.

"It's important to be firm," Ms. Smirt said. "Tough love might just be what these girls need."

"Yeah? All right," he said. "So, there was some talk about cash."

"Yes, your first assistance check will come in the mail in seven to ten days," Smirt replied.

Greeley spit on the ground and cursed. "Well, there goes Atlantic City! Come on, kids. I just got out of the joint and haven't seen my old lady in years. If she plays her cards right, she might be your new mommy."

Sabrina took her sister's hand and allowed Mr. Greeley to lead them to his pickup truck.

"Don't come back, girls," Ms. Smirt said with a wicked smile.

The sisters climbed into Greeley's truck as he gunned the engine, then whipped it into fourth gear and let the wheels spin until they burned tracks on the ground. He chuckled to himself, proud of this display, then shifted back into first gear.

"All right, let's get into some trouble," he said.

He drove through the city with reckless abandon, making hair-pin turns that were far too dangerous for the amount of snow on the ground. He cut people off and ran several red lights as he swore at everyone he saw. He turned one corner and hit a patch of slushy snow, showering ice and filth on an old man with a cane. He blasted his horn and laughed.

"That was mean!" Daphne shouted.

"That's why it was funny," Greeley said.

"You should go back and see if he's OK."

"Yeah, right, kid. You don't go back if you're guilty. That old fool would probably beat me to death with his walking stick. Don't you know nothing?"

"What did you just say?" Sabrina asked. "About not going back."

"Only a numbskull goes back to check on his victims. What would I say to ol' gramps, anyway? He saw me laughing at him. You don't go back to help someone if you meant to hurt them."

Greeley's words bounced around Sabrina's mind. *You don't go back to help someone if you meant to hurt them.*

"Cobweb didn't kill Oberon," Sabrina said to herself.

Daphne turned to her sister. "What did you say?"

"Cobweb came back to check on us when he should have kept running. He thought we might have been hurt. In fact, he came back twice! Guilty people don't come back."

"What the heck are you two babbling about?" Greeley asked.

Daphne ignored him. "He was worried about us."

"He was!"

"But Oberon told us Cobweb killed him," Daphne argued. "Why would he lie?"

"Maybe he wasn't lying. Maybe he was just wrong. Cobweb was the last person to see him. And he gave him the poisoned wine, but who gave the wine to Cobweb?"

"You think someone used Cobweb and made it look like he was guilty?"

"It's possible! No, it's more than possible. I think it's probably what happened. Remember when we asked Oberon and Cobweb about the Scarlet Hand? Neither one of them knew what it was, yet its mark ended up on Oberon's body. Someone had to put it there, and if Cobweb isn't a member, it has to be someone else!"

"Hey! Why don't you go back to the no-talky-talky that you were doing when we met? You're givin' me a migraine," Greeley complained.

"We've got to find Granny," Daphne said. "Right?"

Sabrina looked into her sister's eyes. She knew what the little girl was really asking. She wanted Sabrina to change her mind about retiring. She wanted Sabrina to see what a great detective she could be. Sabrina had to admit there was something about putting the clues together that gave her a funny little thrill. Still, the danger outweighed the excitement.

"One thing at a time, Daphne," she said, tilting her head toward Greeley.

The truck stopped at a red light, and before Sabrina knew what was happening, Daphne had jumped out of the car. Sabrina was quick to follow. The girls had pulled this trick a hundred times, but Sabrina always took the lead. It felt odd, but Sabrina knew her little sister was growing up.

"You come back here!" Greeley shouted as he leaped out of his truck.

Daphne raced ahead, but Sabrina slipped on the ice and fell to the pavement. Before she could scramble to her feet, Greeley was yanking her up by her hair.

"Let's go get your sister," he said, pulling her along with one hand and carrying a crowbar in the other. They crossed a street, then ducked into an alley. Unfortunately, Daphne had led them all into a dead end. Sabrina watched her sister spin around in panic.

"I'm sorry," she said.

Greeley tossed Sabrina at her sister's feet. Then he smacked his crowbar into the palm of his hand. It made a sickening sound.

"What did I say? What did I say?" he growled. "I said it's my way or the highway."

"I guess we took the highway," Sabrina said, rubbing her sore head.

"Now we've got a problem," Greeley said. "You see, I've got me a temper, and when I get angry I do things I regret."

"Don't take another step toward us!" Sabrina shouted.

"See, this is what I'm talking about. I don't want no guff, you little brat," Greeley said. "Didn't they tell you I've killed seven people?"

"Is that all?" a voice said from above. Sabrina looked up and saw a huge figure dropping out of the sky. He landed on the ground hard, cracking the cement underneath him. When he stood, Sabrina smiled. It was Mr. Canis. "Hardly a number I'd brag about."

Greeley took a step back, but then he clenched his fists. "Where did you come from? You sure you want to get in my business?" He swung his crowbar threateningly.

"I know I want to get into your business," another voice said from behind the thug. It was Mr. Hamstead.

"I was thinking I'd like to as well," a third voice said from above. It was Bess, floating down from the sky with her rocket pack blasting. She touched down on the ground and the flames went out.

"What are you people?" Greeley screamed.

"We're fairy tales," Mr. Hamstead said. "It's time for your bedtime story."

Hamstead punched Greeley in the face, and the greasy criminal fell over like a tree. Bess walked over and kicked the man as he curled up into a ball. Mr. Canis, on the other hand, stood by looking bored. Sabrina could have watched the beating all day, but a hand was on her shoulder. She turned and found Granny Relda standing behind her. Daphne was hugging the old woman with all her might, but Granny still had a free hand to pull Sabrina into the embrace.

"Come along, girls, we need to leave the city as quickly as possible. I'm afraid I may have gotten the family into a lot of trouble with this incident," Granny replied. "Smirt will surely send the police to arrest me for kidnapping."

"No, Granny, we have to go see Titania," Sabrina said.

"What? Why?"

"She needs to know Cobweb didn't kill Oberon."

When they reached the Golden Egg, Mustardseed was waiting outside Oberon's old office. He led them into the room, where the queen sat solemnly at her husband's desk. She was now wearing a smart pinstriped suit, tailored for her figure but reminiscent of the one Oberon had once worn. She held a framed photo in her hands. She looked exhausted, her eyes bloodshot. It was obvious she had been crying. Oz stood by, watching with concern. When he noticed the group, he waved them off.

"Mustardseed, your mother is having a difficult day," he said. "I'm sure I can handle this business for her."

"No. Step forward, son, and bring your friends," Titania said without looking up. Her eyes were glued to the photo, but she didn't share it with the group. "This was a happy day. We walked through Central Park among the humans. I thought we'd have an eternity of those moments. Now he's gone, and there are so many things I wish I had said."

Titania was quiet for a moment. Though Sabrina was bursting to tell her what she'd discovered, she also knew silence was the best thing she could offer the heartbroken queen.

"I'm told my husband's murderer has been killed," Titania continued. "Your family's reputation for excellent detective work has proved accurate. We owe you a debt of gratitude."

"Even if Cobweb's death steals real justice from our people," Mustardseed said.

"Actually, Cobweb is owed justice as well," Granny said. "We believe he was innocent."

"Indeed?" Oz said.

"My granddaughter has given this some serious thought and has found some interesting questions that don't have answers," the old woman said, gesturing for Sabrina to step forward.

"You are Puck's chosen protector, I understand," Titania said.

Sabrina nodded, sniffing her still-pungent hair. "For better or worse."

"You don't believe Cobweb killed his father?" Titania asked, this time without the rage and hostility of their previous meeting.

Moth entered the room with Puck's chrysalis floating behind her. The fairy girl flashed the Grimms her usual angry look, but the cocoon darted to Sabrina like a dog reunited with its owner.

"What are they doing here?" she snarled.

Sabrina ignored the fairy princess. "We've learned some things about Cobweb that have only led to more questions. First, he was working closely with Oberon to rebuild the kingdom. He told me that he and the king were planning to build a homeless shelter and a clinic. I believe he respected and supported Oberon. So why would he kill the king?"

"You can't believe anything Cobweb said. He was a liar!" Moth insisted.

"Sure, a person can say anything, but how they act is very different. We chased Cobweb all over town attempting to capture him. But twice, when we were nearly killed—in the subway and on Silver's boat—he came back to help. If he was guilty, why come back and risk getting caught? Why would he care if we were safe or not?"

"Those are not the acts of a murderer," Mustardseed said.

Sabrina nodded. "Oberon's ghost told us that Cobweb was the last person he saw before he died. He said Cobweb brought him a glass of wine—the same glass that was poisoned."

"But what if someone poisoned it before Cobweb received it?" Titania whispered.

"In Ferryport Landing, there's a group of people who have caused a lot of trouble," Granny said. "No one here seems to know who they are, but they're responsible for kidnapping my son and daughter-in-law, Veronica Grimm. They left their mark on Oberon's body. Perhaps Oberon's death and Veronica's kidnapping are connected."

"This is growing tedious. What evidence do you have?" Moth asked.

"None," Sabrina said. "But if we find out who poured the glass of wine that killed Oberon—"

The queen shook her head. "And how do you propose to learn that?"

"The same way we learned who gave Oberon the poison," Daphne said. "Scrooge! He talks to ghosts. He could help us talk to Cobweb's spirit. You could come, too. You could have a chance to say good-bye to Oberon."

Titania rose from her chair. "Is this true?"

"Mother, I've heard talk of Scrooge's talents," Mustardseed said. "Suppose the girl is right. Suppose Cobweb is not the true killer. The murderer could still walk among us. Cobweb could reveal his or her name."

"A waste of Your Highness's time," Moth said. "I was there. I believe he is a charlatan. The whole thing is done with smoke and mirrors."

Titania ignored her. "Take me to Scrooge. I'll need a few moments to prepare."

Mustardseed turned to the group. "We'll join you in the restaurant."

Sabrina and the others left the office and headed back down the hallway. Moth followed them and stepped into Sabrina's path, gritting her teeth.

"It appears Puck is happier with you as his protector. Unfortunately, there are a number of practices and sacred tasks that you need to perform before he emerges."

"What kind of tasks?" Sabrina asked.

"They will not take long."

"I really can't," Sabrina argued. "We're leaving any minute. Can it wait?"

"I also thought you would like some time alone with Puck. He's the King of Faerie now. If the kingdom is to be rebuilt, he will have a great deal of responsibility. He'll have to stay with us. You may never see him again."

Sabrina felt something rise in her throat. She'd never considered that Puck might not come back with her family. But of course he would have to stay. His people needed him. Why would he go back to Ferryport Landing and be trapped inside the town again, anyway? She felt like she might cry, then laughed out loud. Cry? Puck was an irritating pain in the behind. He was constantly giving her a hard time, putting slimy things in her bed, dumping her into big vats of sticky glop. They had never shared a meal he didn't ruin with his explosive flatulence. She should have been happy to get rid of him. She would be free of his army of chimpanzees, his pranks, his name calling. Right?

But the kiss. Her first kiss. Why couldn't she just forget that stupid kiss?

"I think we have a few minutes," Granny Relda said. "Go and say good-bye."

"OK," Sabrina said.

Moth led her down the hallway to a room. Once inside, the little fairy closed the door and locked it. "No one can enter during the ceremony."

Puck's chrysalis followed them inside and hovered close to Sabrina. As smelly as it was, it seemed protective of her. She might even miss it floating around her head.

"There is a ceremonial elixir," Moth said. "I will prepare it."

"You do that," Sabrina said impatiently.

Moth approached a table filled with potions and powders and went to work, busily mixing them together in a small ceramic cup.

"On the day of a fairy's emergence from their healing vessel, our people drink a ceremonial toast to a healthy new life. Very few humans have ever been present. This is a great honor," Moth said.

"Well, I'm happy to be included. Can you hurry up, though?" Sabrina asked, then turned to the cocoon. She felt suddenly sad about what she needed to say. "Puck, I've come to say good-bye. You're free from Ferryport Landing. That's something a lot of Everafters and I, myself, would like to be. You're going to stay here with your mother and brother. Apparently, you're the new King of Faerie, so you're going to have to grow up a little. I . . . I never got a chance to say I was sorry for slugging you when you . . . you . . . well you know. I wasn't expecting it, and, well, it wasn't exactly a dream come true for my first . . . to be surrounded by a bunch of tick-eating chimpanzees. I was angry when it happened. But I'm glad it was you."

She could feel her eyes welling up with tears. "OK, enough of that. You take care of yourself and fix this place, all right? It's a mess. I'm going to come back here someday, and if I find out you were a jerkazoid, there's going to be trouble."

Moth returned with two golden goblets lined with glowing jewels. She handed one to Sabrina and raised it for a toast. "To Puck."

"To Puck." Sabrina took a drink. Whatever the ceremonial elixir was, it didn't taste half bad. There was a fruity taste like raspberries, but there was also a hint of honey and oatmeal—and there was something else, something a little bitter that she couldn't quite place.

"So, I suppose you two will be getting married," Sabrina said conversationally.

"Naturally. Once Puck learns it was I who brought his father's killer to justice, he'll of course take me as his bride. He might have had doubts about me in the past, but now that I've proven myself worthy, I believe the marriage will happen quickly."

"Well, don't forget to send me an invitation to the big day," Sabrina said with a sneer.

Moth flashed one back at her.

"To be honest, Princess, I wouldn't be surprised if he showed up back on our front porch," Sabrina said taking another sip of her drink. "He seems to enjoy tormenting me."

Moth set down her glass. "I thought the same thing."

Suddenly, there was a horrible pain in Sabrina's belly. She lost her breath and fought to catch it as a second wave of pain rolled over her. It was so powerful she doubled over and fell to her knees. The goblet of elixir tumbled onto the floor, and the black liquid spilled all over the boards.

"Moth, I'm sick. Go get my grandmother!" Sabrina cried.

"You think you've got his heart, don't you, human? Well, maybe you're right, but I won't stand for it."

Sabrina looked at the cup. Moth had put something in it. Everything was so confusing, and the pain was so intense, like someone stabbing her with a hot knife.

"Imagine my humiliation when Puck rejected me! Imagine the looks people gave me! I was supposed to be the next queen! I held my head high and waited for him to come to his senses. But he never got a chance! His father threw him out of the kingdom."

"Help," Sabrina grunted. Everything was spinning.

"When you and your family brought him back, I thought Oberon would give him another chance, but he refused. As soon as Puck was well, he was to be removed. I knew I had to act. I snatched Cobweb's pouch when he wasn't looking and mixed some potions and powders. I collected the brew in a bottle and stepped back into the celebration. There was food, wine, everything one needs for a proper feast. Cobweb, ever the loyal and attentive servant, ran past me with a goblet of wine. I knew it was for the king. I distracted him and poured the potion into the cup. Moments later, Oberon was dead. I couldn't believe my luck—but then you and your family had to get involved. Well, this time I'm not going to let anything get in my way, especially not some filthy human."

Another stab of pain hit Sabrina in the belly. This time, it migrated up her spine toward her brain. She could barely think straight, and she was too weak to fight back or even call out for help. But there was something going on with the chrysalis. Had she just seen it change shape?

"When they find me, they'll know what you did," Sabrina groaned.

"Do you think I don't have it in me to kill them all?" Moth said.

Sabrina thought she heard a ripping sound. It was becoming difficult to focus.

"Now that Puck is king, we are going to rebuild this kingdom. I've already mapped out most of Central Park. We'll run the humans out and build a proper castle. We'll show the rest of the Everafters who's in charge. They'll bow at our feet."

That ripping sound again. It was coming from behind Moth.

"Then we'll take over the whole city and enslave anyone that tries to stop us," Moth continued.

Sabrina lifted her heavy eyelids and saw a familiar figure looking down at her from behind Moth.

"Grimm, are you in trouble again? I swear, if I had a nickel for every time I had to save your sorry behind, I'd be a rich fairy."

"Puck," she groaned.

"Your Majesty," Moth said as she spun around. "I can explain this—"

But she never finished her sentence. Puck took out his flute and blasted a couple of notes. A stream of pixies soared through the window, swooped down, and lifted Sabrina off the ground.

"What did you do to her, Moth?"

The little princess shook her head. "You don't understand, my love. I did this for us."

Puck noticed the goblet lying on the floor. He picked it up and smelled it. "Now that wasn't very nice." He turned to his pixies. "Find Cobweb. We need his medicine."

There was some buzzing, and Puck's face crinkled in horror.

"My father?"

The pixies twittered on.

"Half of you find my mother. The other half keep an eye on Moth."

The pixies did as they were told, depositing Sabrina in Puck's arms as they set about their tasks. Puck raced to the locked door and kicked it open. Sabrina looked back to see Moth swatting wildly at the little dots of light.

"Hang on, Sabrina," Puck commanded.

The world grew very dim. She heard Puck telling her to stay awake, but she couldn't. She was so tired. She just wanted to sleep. Maybe if she could fall asleep, the pain would go away.

She had a disorienting dream. Puck was standing over her. He morphed into Titania, then melted into Granny Relda, then Daphne, who was crying. *Don't cry, Daphne.* Then Daphne became Canis, who became Hamstead, who became Bess, who became black nothingness.

Sabrina woke up in the dark. No, dark wasn't the right word. There was light, but it was faint and seemed to be coming from behind the walls she was pressed against. The room was so tiny. No, room wasn't the right word. It was a space, small and confined. There wasn't any room to move. She tried to stretch out, but her hands met a cold, damp wall. She reached down and realized she was sitting in fluid, something thick like gravy, and it was halfway up her chest. She started to panic, reaching around for some way to escape. Directly above her, she found what felt like a seam. She pushed against it and it split. A bright light flooded the space, and she forced herself to stand. She was free, squinting against the bright light, and surrounded by people. When her eyes finally adjusted, she realized the people were her family. They stared back at her for a long, quiet moment.

"That was the most disgusting thing I've ever seen," Puck said. "Why don't I carry a camera with me?"

Sabrina looked down at the prison she had just escaped from and fought the urge to barf. She'd been inside her own chrysalis. Granny Relda and Oz rushed to her and wiped away the layers of goop.

"How are you feeling?" Granny asked.

"I feel fine, though I'll never eat eggplant again as long as I live," Sabrina said, looking down at the crushed cocoon.

"The chrysalis removed the toxins from your system and allowed you to heal," Oz explained. "Moth's poisons would have been lethal without it."

"She tried to give you the Oberon treatment," Daphne said, rushing to Sabrina and wrapping her arms around her sister's neck. "The pixies made her confess."

"Where is she?"

"She was arrested. She'll see a judge as soon as we can determine who might be qualified to be one," Mustardseed said. He smiled and turned to his brother. "Our mother is waiting."

"Duty calls," Puck said as he rolled his eyes. He waved to Sabrina and left with his brother.

Granny hugged Sabrina and burst into tears. "I am sorry, Sabrina. I would never forgive myself if you got hurt. I should have protected you."

"This wasn't your fault," Sabrina replied. "We knew Moth was mean, we just didn't know she was homicidal. We need to question her about the Scarlet Hand now. She can tell us things. She might even know who kidnapped Mom and Dad and put the sleeping spell on them."

Granny shook her head. "She confessed to everything. She says she isn't a member of the Scarlet Hand and has never heard of it."

# 9

ON CHRISTMAS EVE MORNING, SABRINA, Daphne, Granny, Canis, Hamstead, Bess, Mustardseed, Puck, Titania, Oz, and a slew of fairies and other Everafters stood on a desolate bank of the Hudson River. Near the shore was a boat carved from the trunk of an enormous tree. Inside, Oberon's body rested, the boat gently rising and falling with the river's waves. A long sword was in his hands and he was wearing a suit of leather armor with a lion painted on the chest plate. Sabrina barely recognized him.

Titania gave a speech, wishing her husband safe passage into the underworld. She placed a red rose, which she said had been grown in the fairy homeland, on his chest, and then she stepped aside. Mustardseed followed, sharing memories of his father: Oberon's bravery in long-ago days, his struggles as his new home in America collapsed, and even his plans to rebuild. He placed a white rose next to his mother's red. Then it was Puck's turn to speak.

"My father was a complicated man—one who maintained

strong traditions. He held unbendable beliefs, and those beliefs often got in the way of new beginnings. He wanted the best for us, but he didn't always know how to make that happen, and he was easily frustrated when we disagreed. As I am the new king, his blood will endure."

Puck tossed a green rose on his father's chest. One of the ogres from the Golden Egg stepped forward with a torch and handed it to Puck. The boy fairy took it and set the boat ablaze. Then he and his brother pushed it out into the water. The flames quickly engulfed the floating casket, and the river carried it away. Soon, it was out of sight.

Oz stepped up to the Ferryport Landing group. "I suppose you'll be leaving soon."

Granny Relda nodded. "We've got to get back home and see if we can wake up the girls' parents."

"I wish you the best of luck," Oz said as he turned to the girls and shook their hands. "It was very nice to meet all of you. I've got to get back to work. It's Christmas Eve, and another one of the robot elves is on the fritz."

As the crowd drifted away, Granny suggested they return to their hotel for some rest before the long drive home. Sabrina said she'd be along in a minute and waited for Puck. He was discussing something with his brother. Mustardseed nodded, and his wings unfurled. He took to the sky and flew away.

Puck didn't notice Sabrina at first, but when he did he quickly wiped his tears on his sleeve and forced a smile. She reached out and took his hand, and they stood looking out at the river in silence.

"So, what do I call you? Your Majesty?"

"You should have been calling me that all along," Puck replied.

"Your speech was very nice," Sabrina said.

"My mother wrote it for me. She didn't care too much for what I came up with myself."

Sabrina smiled. "I'd like to hear the original version."

Puck tilted his head curiously at Sabrina and smiled.

"My father was mean, arrogant, horrible, and selfish. He cared little for anyone and less for those who disagreed with him. His only love was for his precious kingdom."

Puck turned to the burning boat drifting down the river.

"I hated you!" he shouted. "You took every opportunity to remind me that I was a disappointment!"

Suddenly, Puck fell to his knees. Tears streamed down his cheeks. Sabrina rushed to him, knelt down, and used her scarf to wipe them away.

"When I was barely out of diapers, he took me aside and told me I would never be king. He said I was a failure and he would never give up his throne to me. I went to my mother in tears. She said that if he didn't want his own son to rule, then I would have my own kingdom. She called me the Trickster King. It was our secret.

"When I got older, he tried to force me to marry Moth. I told him he was nuts. Disobeying your father is a severe crime in our world. He banished me. But here I am anyway, wearing his crown."

He stood up and wiped his eyes on his sleeve. "If you tell anyone I was crying, you'll regret it, pus brain."

"I won't tell, stinkpot," Sabrina said affectionately. "Looks like you and I finally have something in common."

"What's that?"

"Families we're not sure we want to be part of," Sabrina replied.

"The old lady told me you're quitting," Puck said.

"I don't know what I'm doing. Can you quit something you never wanted to do in the first place?"

"You can't quit something you never tried."

"I tried! But people got hurt when I tried," Sabrina said.

"Poor Sabrina, such a walking disaster," Puck mocked. "I was there. Sure, people got hurt, but if it wasn't for you a lot of us would be dead. Canis, me—I hate to admit it, but we owe you our lives. You're a hero, and as ridiculous as I find it, you're a pretty good one. You help people when no one else can. From what I hear, that's what your mother did, too. It's in your blood, and blood isn't something you can walk away from."

"When did you suddenly become Mr. Maturity?"

Puck laughed. "Don't worry. It won't last." Then he belched in her face. "See! It's over already."

"So, I guess you're going to have to stay," Sabrina said softly.

Before Puck could answer, there was a loud commotion up on the hill overlooking the river. People were shouting and screaming. Puck and Sabrina ran to investigate.

They found Mr. Hamstead lying on the ground and Bess kneeling beside him. Fat Tony was hovering above the couple with clenched fists. Poor Mr. Hamstead had been socked in the eye.

"I told you to leave my girl alone!" Fat Tony yelled.

"And I told you I'm not your girl anymore!" Bess cried.

Mr. Hamstead crawled to his feet. "Bess, I can handle this." He turned to Fat Tony. "Is this how you want to do it? That's fine with me."

The two men rushed at each other, throwing fists and landing horrible blows. Fat Tony was the first to fall, but he quickly got up and knocked Mr. Hamstead into a mud puddle. The portly man fell with a painful thud.

Sabrina spotted Mr. Canis in the crowd. He was watching as if he had no concern for his friend. Sabrina raced to him and tugged on his sleeve. "We have to stop this. Mr. Hamstead is going to get hurt."

Mr. Canis shook his head. "The pig is tougher than he looks, child."

"Fat Tony is twice his size!" Sabrina cried.

"And the Wolf is four times his size, but Hamstead took me down. Have a little faith in the sheriff."

Fat Tony kicked Hamstead mercilessly, forcing him to flounder in the mud. Each time their friend tried to get up, Tony attacked, keeping him on his hands and knees.

"You don't come to my town and steal my girl!" Fat Tony bellowed.

"Leave him alone, Tony!" Bess demanded.

Fat Tony's face twisted into a demented smile. "Not until I teach your friend a lesson." He lifted his leg to deliver another nasty kick, but this time Hamstead caught it. He pulled hard, and Fat Tony fell onto his back. Hamstead leaped onto him, and the two men wrestled.

Then, all at once, Sabrina saw a magic wand appear in Fat Tony's hand.

"Hamstead, look out!" Canis roared.

The sheriff jammed his elbow into Tony's gut. The fairy godfather let out a wheeze and dropped his wand. Hamstead was right on top of him, and the two fought for control of the weapon. They rolled around in the mud, struggling violently. But just as Mr. Hamstead gained the upper hand, a transformation came over him. His arms and legs shrank into stubby hoofed feet. His ears became furry points at the top of his head. In a matter of seconds, Mr. Hamstead's true form was revealed. He was a pig.

But he was a pig with a magic wand in his snout. He flicked his head in a circle, and a beam of magic shot out of the starry tip. It hit Fat Tony with a puff of smoke, and when it disappeared the big fairy godfather was gone, replaced with a beady-eyed rat. The rat twittered, sized up the enormous pig hovering over him, shrieked, and then raced off, disappearing over the hill.

"I told you so," Mr. Canis mumbled.

Sabrina nodded. Mr. Hamstead was a lot more resourceful than she had given him credit for. Daphne raced to the enormous pig and gave him a big hug around the neck.

"I'm so proud of you, Mr. Hamstead," the little girl said.

"Ernie?" The pig looked up, and Sabrina followed his gaze. Bess was standing there, looking confused and shocked. "Ernie, you're a . . ."

"Pig," said Mr. Hamstead as he morphed back to his human form. He stared at his feet and looked as if he wanted to be a million miles away. "I'm a pig, Bess. In fact, I'm one of the Three Little Pigs. I should have told you. It wasn't fair. I just didn't think you'd give me another look if you knew the truth. I'm sorry."

"Ernie, you lied to me," Bess said. Her face told everyone watching that her heart was breaking.

"I'm really sorry." Hamstead turned abruptly, pushed his way through the crowd, and disappeared.

"We should go get him," Daphne said to her grandmother.

"No, *liebling*," Granny said sadly. "He needs some time to himself."

When they got back to the hotel, Mr. Canis decided to meditate while they waited for Hamstead to return. The old man was sure the traffic out of town would test his temper. Granny bought a suitcase so they could pack the few things the family had purchased during their stay in the city, and they ordered a big lunch from room service. Puck came to see them off, and he spent most of the afternoon talking to the numerous pixies who visited the hotel window. He gave them several orders and answered their questions. King Puck was already hard at work.

Sabrina slipped into the bathroom for some privacy. She washed her face, brushed her teeth, and studied herself in the mirror. She had her father's golden hair and blue eyes, but her face was Veronica's. She knew that when she was older she would look a lot like her mother. Yet she worried that was where the similarities ended. She might never understand why her mother had chosen to work with the Everafters. Why had she chosen such a dangerous life if she didn't have to? Her husband wanted nothing to do with being a fairy-tale detective, so what was the attraction? It broke Sabrina's heart to know she might never know the answer. If the family couldn't find a way to wake her parents, Veronica Grimm would forever be a mystery to her.

She took her mother's wallet out of her pocket and opened it. Inside was the picture of Sabrina and Daphne. Next to it was Oz's business card. The wizard claimed he knew Veronica better than anyone, and suddenly Sabrina had an idea. She burst out of the bathroom and found Daphne and Puck finishing off three huge hot fudge sundaes. Granny was sitting in a chair with her feet propped up on an ottoman.

"I want to talk to Oz before we go," Sabrina said to her grandmother.

"Sabrina, I thought you were in a hurry to get back home," Granny said.

"Please! I need to ask him some questions. I need to understand my mother."

Sabrina, Daphne, Granny Relda, and Puck took a taxi to Thirty-fourth Street. It was evening by the time they reached Macy's, and a crowd of exhausted shoppers was flooding out of the doors, but the family managed to squirm their way inside. The store security guard blocked their path, frowned, and tapped his watch. "Christmas Eve, folks. We're closing in five minutes."

"We're not buying anything. We're looking for the Wizard," Sabrina said.

"The who?"

"We're looking for Mr. Diggs," Granny clarified.

"He's probably in his workroom," the guard grumbled. "Just don't dillydally, all right? Some of us would like to go home."

They found Oz's workroom. Sabrina knocked once, but no one answered. She pushed the door open slightly and peered inside, but it was too dark. "Oz? I want to ask you some questions about my mother."

"Perhaps we should wait out here for him," Granny said.

"C'mon," Puck said as he opened the door and pushed Sabrina inside.

"Children, we are intruding," Granny worried.

"He might be in the back and can't hear us," Daphne said, pulling the old woman inside.

The room was as big of a mess as it had been on their last visit. Several tables were full of robot parts, many of which were still moving—including a head that kept opening its eyes and lifting its brows in surprise. Tools littered the room, some of them seeming to have found permanent homes on the floor.

"Ugh, do you smell that?" Puck asked.

"No. What are you talking about?" Sabrina said defensively. She thought the chrysalis smell had finally faded but secretly worried she was just getting used to it.

"I smell hard work in here. It's horrible," Puck said as he picked up a circuit board and examined it. "I might gag."

Sabrina sat down on a stool to wait for the Wizard. She was worried the security guards would lock them inside, but she needed to talk to Oz one last time. When Daphne found her own stool, a robotic head that was sitting on the table next to her sprang to life and started giggling. The little girl screamed and snatched a hammer off the table. She smacked the head a couple of times until it stopped laughing.

"You taught that head a lesson, didn't you, marshmallow?" Puck said as he took the hammer from the little girl. He hit the head himself for good measure and scanned the room for something else to beat on. After a while, he sat down and started peeking through a stack of papers on the desk.

"Don't snoop," Granny Relda scolded.

"Then someone better keep me entertained, 'cause this is boring," Puck replied.

Sabrina got up and snatched the papers away from the fairy. "This is Oz's stuff. Some of it might be private." She tried to collect them in a neat stack, but shoved in the middle of the pile was something quite different: a small, leather-bound journal with gold writing on its cover.

*Fairy-Tale Accounts*
*June 1992 to present*
*Veronica Grimm*

Sabrina couldn't believe it. This was her mother's journal! But what was it doing here in Oz's lab?

"What did you find?" Granny Relda asked.

"It's my mother's journal," Sabrina replied as she opened it with trembling fingers. Veronica's curved, slightly sloppy script filled every page. There were hundreds of entries chronicling her experiences with the Everafters of both Ferryport Landing and New York City. Sabrina read feverishly, turning pages faster and faster, absorbing as much as she could about her mother's secret life. There was story after story of the lives Veronica had changed. She helped people move, helped them find jobs and track down missing friends, and she had done plenty of detective work as well. On one of the pages she wrote:

*My work with these people is exciting, fascinating, and most of all—important. I've found that there is more to being a Grimm than Henry ever told me. It's more than being a detective . . . Sometimes, I'm the only hope an Everafter has of making it in this world.*

*If only I could get them to work together . . .*

Sabrina flipped to the back and found several folded pages from a yellow legal pad, covered with writing. She read through them, including all the scratched-out parts and tiny notes in the margins. It was a speech.

"This is the speech everyone was talking about. It was her plan for the Everafters. She was supposed to give it the day she disappeared," Sabrina said.

"Then what is Oz doing with it?" Daphne asked, taking the journal from her sister.

Granny got up from her chair. "*Lieblings*, I think it would be wise of us to—"

Oz stepped into the light. "Your mother was a remarkable woman, girls. Her charisma was almost, well, supernatural. She could convince people to do anything she wanted. Your mother collected an army of supporters using only her smile. It was a talent I always envied. I had to use fear a lot of the time to get things done.

"She had an incredible influence on me. I loved the little adventures we used to go on. She was part saint and part detective, running around helping people, and for a while I thought I could be like her, too. But then I would come into work every day, and have my boss criticize the displays even though their inner workings were beyond anything his little brain could conceive. I'd get my measly paycheck and head back to my tiny apartment in Queens, and I'd look up at the stain on the ceiling above my bed. It was shaped like Oz. Can you believe it? One morning I woke up and the light was coming in the window just right and that stain glowed green. It dawned on me that my life had taken a terrible turn. I was once the Great and Terrible Oz! I'd ruled a nation of fairies and talking animals and witches and magical creatures. They had feared me, yet somehow I had become a nobody. I ran around fixing Oberon's problems and working on these stupid robots."

He picked up the head on his work table and tossed it into the dark, where it landed with a crash.

"I thought I was doomed to live that life forever, but one day I met a man who offered me something more. He has plans, folks. I'm going to be part of them—a new vision for the entire world, where Everafters rule and humans cower in fear. In this bright future, there will be a need for experienced leaders like myself. All I had to do was join the Scarlet Hand."

Sabrina gasped. "Then you killed Oberon. You put the mark on his chest!"

"Oh, I'm no murderer. Moth killed him. I just took advantage of his death to announce the coming of the Master's army."

"Let me guess. You and the 'Master' are going to take over the world, right? You know, as a villain myself, I have to admit the whole conquering routine is getting old," Puck said.

"It's the only way to put things right, Your Majesty, and if you're smart, you'll join us. The humans have controlled things for long enough, and look at what they've done with their time. This planet is a cesspool of pollution, hate, and greed. It's a world of small ideas and tiny imaginations."

"I think I'll pass. I actually enjoy a good cesspool," Puck said.

"And Henry and Veronica were in the way," Granny Relda said.

"You kidnapped our parents!" Daphne gasped.

"Unfortunately, yes, but it wasn't an easy choice. I lured them out, promising your mother I would help her with her speech and encouraging her to reveal her double life to your father. Once I had them, I turned them over to the Master."

"And what do you get for betraying them?" Sabrina demanded.

"I get to build a new Emerald City on top of this one."

Suddenly, there was a loud bang as lights went off in the building. The security guards were closing the store.

"Now, about Veronica's journal. You can keep it, but there's a speech inside that I need. Give it to me, and you and your family can go back to Ferryport Landing unharmed. Your family's usefulness to the Master is over, and if you go now you'll have time to find a place to hide when the army comes."

"That's very kind of you," Granny said. "But I think we're going to hang on to it."

The Wizard reached into his pocket and removed his small, silver remote. "Why is everyone in your family so stubborn?" He pushed a button, and at once every little robot head turned toward them with blazing electrical eyes. The machines charged at them, some dragging half-assembled bodies. Puck swatted a few away with his wooden sword, but one of the mechanical birds swooped down and snatched the journal right out of Sabrina's hand. It immediately flew back to Oz and gave him its prize. He flipped through the pages, found the speech, and ran.

The family fought through the crowd of misfit robots as Oz dashed out of the workroom and through the dark, empty store. A few security lights lit the way, but he kept overturning racks of clothing and merchandise in the family's path.

Puck stopped short and quickly transformed into a bull with long horns. He bent his head down and charged forward, tossing the obstacles out of the way. The Grimms raced close behind.

They watched Oz take the escalator up to the floor above. Puck transformed back to his normal state to run up the moving stairs. Sabrina wasn't far behind. Daphne stayed back to help Granny along.

The duo chased Oz up five flights. They were racing through the dark store when something huge and hulking came around the corner at them. It was a seven-foot-tall Nutcracker, painted with a red coat and white beard. Its most horrible feature was a gaping mouth that clamped shut every few moments. It punched Puck and he flew across the store and slammed into a wall.

"Oh dear," Granny said as she and Daphne came up behind Sabrina.

Puck got to his feet, rushed behind the Nutcracker, and delivered a well-placed kick to its behind. The robot turned and lunged at him.

"They don't sell explosives in this store, do they?" Puck

shouted as he dodged the creature's massive arm. "Maybe some dynamite?"

"They sell everything else," Sabrina said, glancing at a store directory on the wall. "Wait a minute. Sporting goods! We're on the sporting goods floor!"

With the monster's attention on Puck, Sabrina and her family searched for weapons. Daphne found a tennis racket, which she swung wildly at the robot, but one bite of the Nutcracker's deadly jaws turned it into splinters.

Granny found a couple of soccer balls, but when she tossed them at the monstrosity, one bounced off and the other landed in its mouth, popping with an ear-splitting *BANG!*

"What's that thing?" Puck asked. He pointed to an odd machine that said PITCHMASTER on the side. The contraption shot baseballs through a tube at super high speeds to teach batters how to hit fastballs. *Fastballs!* Sabrina flipped the machine on and pushed a button. A baseball rocketed out of the tube and hit a nearby mannequin, knocking its head off its shoulders.

"Oh, I've got to get me one of those things!" Puck said, pushing her aside so he could take the controls. "Do you think it will shoot balloons filled with donkey poo?"

Sabrina ignored Puck's disgusting idea. "Help me turn this toward the Nutcracker!"

When the machine was aimed at their target, Sabrina hit the

button again and a ball shot out of the tube. It hit the Nutcracker in the shoulder with a force so incredible it knocked an arm right off its body.

The creature turned, a red light flashing in its eyes. It stomped toward them as they took turns firing balls. One crashed into the robot's face, knocking a metal panel off and revealing its internal wiring. Another slammed into its right leg. Each ball knocked the robot back a little, but each time it recovered.

While Puck fired, Sabrina scanned the Pitchmaster's controls. There was a button that read LIGHTNING FASTBALL. She pushed it just as the Nutcracker's hand reached out for her. A ball shot out of the machine and hit the creature between the eyes. Smoke and sparks billowed out of its head. A second later the creature toppled over, shook wildly, then lay still.

"You're out!" Puck cried.

There was a loud clang, and Sabrina turned. Oz was hiding nearby and had knocked over a rack of bicycles in his effort to escape. He raced to the escalators, and the entire family took off after him again. As soon as the Wizard reached the top of one escalator, he hurried to the next until he reached the top floor of the store. When the Grimms and Puck finally got there, he was nowhere in sight.

"Oz, we know you're up here," Granny Relda called out.

"Yeah, you can't hide from us or from the beating you're going to get when we find you," Puck said.

"Shut up! You're not helping," Sabrina said.

"Don't tell me to shut up. I'm a king," Puck said.

"You're an idiot."

An enormous, glowing head materialized out of thin air. It seemed to be made of emerald green fire. Its horrible black eyes focused on the group, and when its mouth opened, Oz's voice bellowed out. "I have never had luck with children. I have to admit, I've always underestimated them and they have been my undoing."

"Aw, shut up." Puck snatched a giant candy cane decoration off a nearby wall and swung it at the head. The cane passed right through it. The head was a hologram.

"Take Dorothy for example," the head continued. "She showed up at the palace with those three idiots asking for ridiculous things. She was dumber than a box of rocks. 'Send me back to Kansas.' If you could have a wizard grant you a wish, would you waste it on going to Kansas? And her friends! 'Give me a heart.' 'Give me a brain.' 'Give me courage.' What they needed was a clue. So I sent them to see the Wicked Witch of the West. Who would have thought they'd ever come back? They ruined everything for me. Well, I won't let it happen again. It's time the Wizard got a wish of his own."

"You're not going to get away with this," Sabrina muttered, looking around the room for Oz's hiding place. In the original story, Dorothy discovered the Wizard was a hoax when she found him huddling behind a curtain while doing the same giant head trick.

"Oh, but I am," the Wizard cried as the head followed her. "After all, I'm the Great and Terrible Oz. I can do magic, child."

The family seemed to have the same suspicions as Sabrina, so while Oz babbled on about himself and his friend, the Master, they poked around the racks and shelves of the store. Sabrina found Oz standing in plain view next to a display for a fancy blender. He was so busy pounding frantically at the buttons on his silver remote control, he didn't even notice her.

Sabrina cleared her throat. "I found him," she shouted to her family.

Oz groaned. "Don't look behind the curtain," he said with an uncomfortable laugh.

"Give me the book," Sabrina said.

"I can't, child," he said, as he pushed a button on his remote. "It would jeopardize the Master's plans. Nothing can get in his way. Not even my best friend's children." Suddenly there was an incredible rumbling from below. The building shifted as a fissure opened at their feet, snaking across the entire floor. Puck and the Grimms were knocked to their knees. The ground was splitting in two to make way for something big, round, and green. It rose higher and higher, and got bigger and bigger, until it nearly filled the entire space. Sabrina suddenly understood what it was—a hot air balloon—and with nowhere else to go, it pushed through the ceiling, causing concrete and wood to crash down around everyone.

A large woven basket rose up from below, and Oz climbed inside as it rose into the open sky.

"Give me the journal, Oz!" Sabrina cried.

"You know the story, Sabrina. You can have your heart's desire, but you have to do something for me. You have to kill the Wicked Witch of the West!" Sabrina saw Oz push another button on his controller just as the balloon disappeared from sight.

"I don't think he's my favorite anymore," Daphne said.

"Don't worry. I'll get him," Puck cried as his wings appeared, but the floor shook so hard he couldn't find the balance to rise. It seemed as if the entire building was rocking back and forth. Then, all at once, the shaking stopped.

"Uh, what was that?" Sabrina said.

Granny looked around nervously. "I don't know, and I don't like it. I think we should get out of here as quickly as possible. Puck, forget the journal. Help me get the girls to safety."

The old woman grabbed Daphne and Sabrina by the hands and hurried them over to the emergency exit. Puck ran after them, and together the group raced down nine flights of stairs.

What they found at the bottom was a disaster. Racks of clothing and broken bottles of perfume were scattered over the floor, and hosiery was draped everywhere. Worst of all, an enormous canyon had opened in the middle of the cosmetics department.

"Find an exit, children," Granny said. But before they could take a step, a big, black, metallic cone began to rise out of the breach in the floor, just the like the balloon before it.

"This can't be good," Puck said.

It crashed through the ceiling, rising higher and higher. Soon the enormous cone was completely revealed, but beneath it came another object. This part was a sickly green face. There was a pair of eyes, one covered in a black patch. Then came a long, pointy, wart-covered nose. Then a mouth full of enormous, jagged fangs. Sabrina grabbed her sister and her grandmother, shook them until they took their eyes off the growing horror, and together with Puck they ran for the closest door.

"What is that thing?" Puck shouted.

"It's a robotic Wicked Witch of the West!" Sabrina shouted back.

Granny pushed hard on the exit door, but it was locked tight.

"They must lock the doors from the outside when they close the store," she said as she scanned the increasingly smaller space for an escape. The higher the robot rose, the more space it took up.

Sabrina pounded on the glass, hoping it would shatter, but she wasn't strong enough. Thankfully, Puck understood the situation.

His arm morphed into a gorilla's, and he punched the door with all his might. It flew off its hinges, and the family raced out into the snow.

Unfortunately, they were not alone. The streets were packed with people. Taxis, trucks, and cars were everywhere. None of them seemed to notice that Macy's was falling apart. Sabrina realized how much easier it was to handle these types of disasters in Ferryport Landing, where the downtown area was usually deserted. But here, in New York City, every corner was as crowded as a parade.

"Run!" Granny Relda yelled to the crowds, and the family took off down the sidewalk, hoping people would follow.

"Get off the streets!" Sabrina shouted. "There's a monster!"

People ignored her and went about their business, but she continued trying to get their attention. "There's a giant robot coming! Run for your lives!"

The family quickly reached the street corner. The traffic was intense, so they couldn't just run out into the crosswalk. They were forced to wait for the light, which gave Sabrina a chance to look back at the store. She did so just in time to see the entire front of the building collapse as a huge leg stepped through. That finally got the New Yorkers' attention. A taxi crashed into a newspaper stand. A bus smacked into a pretzel cart and sent it skidding into the road. Panicked screams rose up from the crowd of pedestrians.

When the light changed, the family raced across the street, continuing to shout warnings at everyone they saw. Sabrina heard a huge pounding noise and looked back again. The robot was completely free of the store now. It stood nearly six stories tall. It gave itself a shake like a wet dog and sent debris flying in every direction. It scanned the streets until it fixed its horrible electronic gaze on the family, then it charged in their direction, kicking a taxicab out of its way. The cab slammed into a light pole.

The family kept running, but now the pedestrians were getting smart. The crowd stampeded to get out of the way, racing around the family in hopes of saving their own lives. A young woman knocked Daphne to the ground in her panic but kept running. Puck helped the little girl up before she was trampled.

"I think this one is going to take more than a few fastballs to knock down!" Puck yelled.

"Look!" Daphne said, pointing above them. Sabrina saw Oz's hot-air balloon sailing into the sky. It was strangely close to the Empire State Building. In fact, it was too close. The spire at the top caught the balloon strings and tangled them tight.

"Oz can stop this thing!" Sabrina shouted. "His remote controls it. Head for the Empire State Building!"

The family raced up the street as the enormous witch grew closer with each giant step. By the time they got to the legendary building, the robot was right on top of them. They pushed through the revolving doors and dashed into the bronze-covered lobby.

A security guard got up from his desk and held up his hand. "We're closed, folks. Come back next week."

"We've got to get to the top now," Sabrina said.

"No can do, people . . ." he said, his voice trailing off. His attention was suddenly on something else. Sabrina turned to follow his gaze and saw the witch robot's good eye staring through the front doors. A second later, its enormous hand smashed through the front doors and snaked across the lobby. Greedy fingers reached for the Grimms.

Sabrina did the first thing that popped into her head. She dragged her family past the security guard and into the waiting elevator at the end of the hall. She scanned the dozens of buttons and found the one she wanted—OBSERVATION DECK. The doors closed and the elevator started to rise.

"You know, I lived in this city for years and I've never been to the top," Puck said. "I hope the souvenir shop is still open."

The elevator came to a stop, and when the doors opened, a blast of cold air and snow hit their faces. Through it, they could just see the outline of a hot-air balloon, caught on top of the building. Oz was frantically trying to unfasten several ropes wrapped around the building's spire as his basket swayed dangerously in the wind, dumping some of its contents onto the roof of the building.

"Turn the witch off!" Sabrina shouted.

Oz looked down and snarled.

"Mr. Diggs, someone is going to get hurt," Granny added. "That is, if they haven't already."

"What do I care if a bunch of humans die? The Master has promised me that I will rule over them all. A few lives mean nothing to me."

Sabrina looked over the edge of the building. The witch was climbing the facade, digging her huge hands into the building's concrete frame. It reminded Sabrina of a movie she'd once seen about a giant ape.

"Oz, you told me you were my mother's best friend," she called out to the Wizard. "She trusted you. Regardless of your plans, I don't think you wanted to hurt her."

"I didn't. The Master told me your parents were part of a bigger plan. He said they'd give birth to the future."

Sabrina glanced down again. The witch was halfway up the building, but Oz paid no attention. He continued to cut his ropes one by one.

"You have a chance to do the right thing," she shouted, but he ignored her.

Puck's wings popped out of his back and flapped fiercely. "If you try to fly away from here, I will blast a hole in your little balloon. I swear it."

Puck's threat didn't seem to faze the Wizard. He cut the last rope and waved good-bye. The balloon, free, drifted skyward. In a flash, Sabrina did something she never would have guessed she had the courage to do. She grabbed the loose rope.

Her brain told her it was stupid—in fact, it was begging her to let go—but she refused, even as her feet were yanked off the roof and she rose higher and higher into the air. She knew what she was doing was insane. She knew she might die, but Oz had to be stopped.

"Let go, you foolish child!" Oz shouted from above. Sabrina could see he was struggling to untie the rope she was holding onto, without success.

"Turn off the robot!" Sabrina cried, pulling herself hand over hand up the rope.

"This is all pointless, Sabrina. You can't fight the Master or me. The future is coming. Now let go."

"No!" Sabrina had reached the basket. She grabbed onto the side. "Turn it off and tell me how to wake up my parents! You were my mother's best friend. Help me help her!"

The Wizard's face filled with sorrow. "I'm sorry, Sabrina." He pushed her, and she lost her grip. She snatched at his hands before she fell, managing to take his silver remote control, but what good would it do her now? What good would it do anyone?

Wind filled her ears like a lion's roar as gravity pulled her toward the ground.

# 10

"SABRINA!"

Someone was shouting her name over the wind.

"Sabrina. I've got you!"

Suddenly, she wasn't falling anymore. Puck's arms were wrapped around her, and he was grinning.

"That was so dumb, I'm almost proud of you," he continued as he flew them back to the roof of the building. The robot witch was there, practically on top of Relda and Daphne. Panicked, Sabrina pointed the little silver controller at the monster and pushed at the dozen buttons. Just as the robot was about to squash her family, it froze.

Puck eased them down next to Granny and Daphne. Her little sister was in hysterics and hugged Sabrina tighter than ever. Granny joined the hug. She was shaken, as well.

"Come on, people!" Puck said. "Did you really think I was going to let her die?"

Daphne pulled away from Sabrina for a moment. She sniffled and then held out something to her sister. "This fell out of the balloon."

It was their mother's journal. Sabrina opened it, and in the back was the speech that promised to change everything. By the light of the witch's still-glowing eye, she read it to herself. A proud smile spread across her face. She handed it to Granny, who read it as well.

"I think the Everafters should hear this," the old woman said.

"Give it to Puck. He can read it to them, if he agrees."

"*Liebling*, these are your mother's words. They must come from you."

Sabrina met her grandmother's gaze, lifted her chin, and nodded. "OK. We need to get everyone together. Puck, how do we turn this building bright purple?"

Daphne looked at the destruction the witch had caused. Down in the street, thousands of people gathered to look up at the strange monster hanging off one of the city's tallest buildings. "Granny, we're going to need an awful lot of forgetful dust," the little girl said.

Sabrina sat in a back room at the Golden Egg, studying her mother's writing. Daphne was behind her, brushing Sabrina's long blond hair. It helped to calm them both. Sabrina fretted over every syllable and comma, hoping she could somehow do the speech justice. She was not one for talking in front of people, especially in front of Everafters.

"You'll be awesome," Daphne promised. "I'll be standing right next to you."

"Good," Sabrina answered. "You can deflect the pies and rotten tomatoes they toss at me."

"I think that only happens in cartoons," Daphne replied. "But I'll keep an eye out for them."

The door opened, and Mustardseed appeared. "They are ready for you."

"We're coming," Daphne said, and he stepped back out to wait in the hall.

"Do I really have to do this?" Sabrina asked. "What if I screw it up? What if I ruin what Mom was trying to do?"

"You won't," Daphne said as she pulled her sister to her feet. "And even if you do, your hair looks fabulous."

"Thanks."

"For a jerkazoid," Daphne added with a smile.

They joined Mustardseed in the hallway. He led them into the restaurant, where they found Puck addressing a huge crowd. He was wearing a jeweled crown and an oversized purple robe, and carrying an enormous scepter. He strolled back and forth, trying to seem dignified while struggling with his outfit.

"Attention!" he shouted. "As you know, there's been some trouble in the last few days. My father, your leader, is dead. I have returned to the kingdom to rule."

"Get on with it, Puck!" one of the dwarfs shouted. "We lost patience with you nearly half an hour ago."

"Now, I know they are terribly ugly and difficult to look at," Puck said, causing Sabrina to growl, "but these girls have got something to say. When they are done, you fools can go back to fighting if you want."

Puck gestured to Sabrina and Daphne. The girls stepped onto the stage and stared at the crowd.

"Good luck," Puck said. "They're a disrespectful bunch."

Sabrina looked down at her mother's speech and stepped to the edge of the stage. Daphne stood next to her. Granny, Canis, and Hamstead were in the crowd, eager to hear what she had to say.

"This was written by my mother," she said.

"We can't hear you!" someone shouted.

"Speak up!"

Sabrina looked to her sister for help.

"You may not talk a lot, but you've never had a problem with volume," Daphne whispered.

Sabrina cleared her throat and started again. "This was written by my mother, Veronica Grimm, on the eve of her disappearance almost two years ago."

Suddenly, the crowd was silent. "I'm afraid I will probably never be the speaker my mother was, but I will read it word for word. It outlines her ideas for you. I hope it helps."

Sabrina looked at her mother's writing, studying the curves of her letters, trying to understand the mind that wrote the words.

"I will not stand here and claim to know your hearts. You have difficult lives. You've seen dreams ripped apart. You've watched as suffering came like floodwaters. I am human. I am blessed. I live in a world that believes in me. Your very existence defies what humanity can accept. You are supposed to be bedtime stories—not flesh and blood. Thus, you live in the shadows, accepting what table scraps you can find and yearning for the life humans take for granted.

"It doesn't have to be like this. You are few, but together you are mighty. Combining your talents, working for one another's benefit, lifting one another up when you fall—this is the path to your happiness. If you worked together as a community, you could build an empire with your small numbers, but instead you choose to squabble and divide yourselves. Well, I say it's time to put hatred aside and hold your brothers' and sisters' hands. You don't need humanity to believe in you. You only need to believe in one another."

Sabrina continued reading. She did her best to make eye contact with people in the crowd, and she held Daphne's hand for support. She could feel her mother's thoughts inside her, Veronica's feelings about every word she put down on the paper. Her mother described a world Everafters could embrace. It was a simple plan based on common sense and a common purpose. She described a government where majority ruled but a passionate minority could not be trampled. She recommended that leaders be elected rather than born. She talked of schools and hospitals. She spoke of science and technology helping the Everafters keep pace with the modern world. Mostly, she spoke of finding common ground.

"You are all Everafters," Sabrina concluded. "Your neighbor's needs are your needs. His passions are your passions, and his heartbreak is your heartbreak. If you can treat his struggles as your own, you will celebrate your successes together. It doesn't matter if he is feathered or furry. It makes no difference if he is on two legs or twenty. Don't waste time finding differences. When you talk to your neighbors, close your eyes and you will truly see them."

After Sabrina spoke the last words, she thanked the crowd and stood back, wondering if they would choose her mother's ideals over their own isolation and mistrust. For a long moment, there was silence. Sabrina looked to Puck and Daphne and Granny Relda, but they were as trapped in the moment as she.

And then Mother Goose stood up. "Thank you, Sabrina Grimm. You serve your family well," she said, and she began to

clap. Others joined her, and soon the entire audience was on its feet applauding: Yahoos, dwarfs, pirates, fairies, and goblins alike. Moments later, a familiar chant began.

"Grimm! Grimm! Grimm!"

Tears ran down Sabrina's cheeks. They weren't tears of sadness but of great pride. Their mother had tried to build something important, and though she wasn't here to see it come to life, Sabrina would tell her when they woke her up. For Sabrina, it was the first time since discovering her family history that she truly understood it. Being a Grimm wasn't just being a fairy-tale detective. It was being the person who helps when no one else can. Being a Grimm was something to be proud of, not something to run from.

Granny Relda pulled the girls close to her.

"I'm ready to be part of this family," Sabrina said.

"I never had any doubts, child," the old woman said as a tear rolled down her cheek. "I never had any doubts."

Daphne hugged her sister tightly. "I'm glad you're back. I can't do this without you."

When the family found their car, it was parked beneath three feet of snow. Mustardseed blasted it with a little fire, and it was clean and clear in no time. Mr. Canis got in awkwardly. His transformation into a wolflike state continued, and he was once again furry and seven feet tall. Getting behind the wheel proved difficult, but he managed. He started the car's engine and let it idle while the family said their good-byes.

Hamstead hadn't spoken to anyone that morning. As he stood on the sidewalk, he shuffled his feet and looked down at the pavement. Sabrina understood. His broken heart wasn't going to mend soon, and neither was hers. She was working hard to hide her sadness that Puck wasn't coming back to Ferryport Landing with the Grimms. Worse still, he hadn't bothered to come and say goodbye to her.

"You've given us some hope for the future," Mustardseed said to her.

"Oh? Well, good luck," Sabrina said, trying to give him her full attention. She kept peering down both ends of the street, hoping to see Puck's shaggy head of hair bouncing in her direction. "Don't let your brother ruin everything. If he has his way, he'll turn the city into a junkyard he can play in all day."

"Yes, I've already found that one in the suggestion box," Mustardseed said. "I am not worried. The Trickster King has plans of his own."

"Well, it's a shame he couldn't be here this morning, but I understand the kingdom needs him. We have matters to attend to ourselves back home," Granny said to the girls. "Sabrina and Daphne start their training bright and early tomorrow morning."

"Training?"

"Yes, detective training," Granny said.

"What have we been doing all this time?" Daphne asked.

"Following me around and getting in trouble," the old woman said. "Now that you both are ready and willing, we're going to explore what's inside the Hall of Wonders. There is a lot to learn if you want to be proper fairy-tale detectives."

Granny Relda and the girls got into the car. Hamstead followed, and they all rolled down their windows and waved goodbye to Mustardseed. Mr. Canis pulled away from the curb to a symphony of backfires and rattles, and pointed the old jalopy north. Sabrina watched out the window as the city rolled past. She saw her father's favorite movie theater, and the place where her mother loved to buy secondhand books. There was the grocer with the yummy plums and the diner that made egg creams. Someday, she promised herself, she would come back here, but for now there was no hurry. She and Daphne had a place to call home.

Suddenly, there was a tapping sound on the roof of the car. Sabrina craned her neck but couldn't see anything. She assumed it was just another of the car's many rattles and thumps, but when the pounding got louder, followed by a fiery blast, Canis slammed on the brakes. When the smoke cleared, there was a beautiful woman wearing a rocket pack and standing with her hands on the hood.

"Bess?" Mr. Hamstead said.

"Ernie! You can't go!"

Mr. Hamstead looked bewildered. He got out of the car tentatively, and everyone else followed.

"I was a fool, Ernie!" Bess cried. "If you leave me, I'll never recover."

"Bess, what are you doing here?"

"I came to tell you I love you. I don't care about your secret. It doesn't matter to me that you're a pig," the woman declared, rushing to Mr. Hamstead and taking his hand. "I was just surprised. I think you're awful adorable in your real body."

"Bess, I don't know what to say," the man said, fumbling for words.

"Say you love me, too."

"I . . . I do love you," Mr. Hamstead said. "But it would never work."

"Why not?" Bess demanded.

"Because I'm an animal and you're . . . you're . . ."

Before he could finish, Bess took a step back and suddenly went through a transformation of her own; only Bess became something quite different. She was a cow.

"You're the most beautiful thing I've ever seen," Hamstead said, finishing his thought.

"Ernie, we're perfect for each other. You're one of the Three

Little Pigs, and I'm the Cow That Jumped Over the Moon," Bess said.

Daphne's palm quickly went into her mouth as Bess the Cow lifted off the ground and zipped around Ernest like an enormous lovesick honeybee.

Hamstead grinned from ear to ear and clapped wildly.

"Stay here with me, cowboy!" she begged.

"I love you, baby!" he cried.

Bess drifted down to the pavement and morphed back into her human form. She rushed to Hamstead's side.

"So I can keep you?" she asked.

Hamstead turned to Granny Relda and hugged her. "What will you tell the community about their missing sheriff?"

Granny shrugged. "Let me worry about it. I couldn't be happier for you. Stay here with Bess and be happy."

"So where are you crazy kids going on your honeymoon?" Daphne asked, wrapping her arms around Hamstead's generous middle.

Everyone laughed.

"I'm thinking Hawaii," Bess said, causing Hamstead's face to spontaneously morph into his pig form.

"Or Paris," he oinked, then pulled himself together. "There's a lot to see, and I've got a bit of cabin fever, if you know what I mean."

He turned to Mr. Canis. "Take care of yourself, Wolf."

Canis nodded and shook Hamstead's hand. "It has been an honor, Pig."

As the group celebrated, Hamstead pulled Sabrina and Daphne aside. "Girls, I fear that things are not going well with our old friend, Mr. Canis. Your grandmother has always had a lot of faith in his self-control, but I believe the Wolf will show his face before too long, no matter how hard Canis fights," he said as he removed a chain from around his neck. There was a small silver key attached to it. He slipped it over Daphne's head and urged her to hide it under her shirt.

"What's this?" the little girl asked.

"Call it Plan B. It opens a safe-deposit box at the town bank. You'll find a weapon inside . . . something powerful enough to stop the Wolf if he goes on a rampage. Mr. Boarman and Mr. Swineheart can help you use it if things get bad. Don't let it fall into the wrong hands, and don't tell anyone you have it. It could be devastating to the town."

"I'll give this to Granny," Daphne said, patting the key.

"No," Hamstead whispered. "Keep it to yourself."

"But—"

"Just trust me."

After Sabrina, Daphne, Granny Relda, and Mr. Canis said their good-byes to Mr. Hamstead and Bess, they got into the car, gave a farewell honk, and drove away. Sabrina settled into her seat and realized she was feeling depressed. When she had heard the thumping on the roof of the car, she'd been sure it was Puck.

Daphne seemed to read her mind. "You know, I really can't believe Puck. What a jerkazoid," she said. "So what if he's a king? He's going to be lousy at it! He should have come back to Ferryport Landing with us."

"What do I care," Sabrina said, trying to hide her feelings. "I say, good riddance to King Smells-a-Lot."

Daphne gazed out the back window, then let out a startled laugh.

"Are you sure about that?" She nudged Sabrina to take a look as well. When she turned in her seat, she was shocked by what she saw. Following not far behind them was the six-story mechanical Wicked Witch of the West. Perched on the top of its hat was Puck, holding a little silver remote in his hand.

"What are those words he spray-painted on the robot's chest?" Daphne asked.

Sabrina smiled. "It says, *Ferryport Landing or Bust*!"

"He's following us home!" Daphne cried.

Granny turned in her seat and smiled. "I believe he is, *liebling*."

"And he's bringing a toy with him," Mr. Canis grumbled.

"I think we're going to need an awful lot of forgetful dust," Sabrina said, and for once she didn't try to hide her smile.

ENJOY THIS
SNEAK PEEK FROM

5

# THE SISTERS GRIMM

## ~ MAGIC AND OTHER ~
## MISDEMEANORS

# 1

I'M SURE THIS COULD BE CONSIDERED CHILD ABUSE," Sabrina groaned. How many children had grandmothers who woke them up by banging a metal pot with a spoon? Granny Relda was like a member of the world's most annoying marching band.

"Sorry, *liebling*, but this is the only way to wake your sister," Granny replied in her light German accent. "Up and at 'em!"

Sabrina rolled over and eyed her seven-year-old sister, Daphne. The two of them had shared a bed for some time now, and Sabrina was well aware of how soundly her little sister slept. Daphne could doze undisturbed through a category-five hurricane, so Granny was forced to resort to unusual methods to wake her. It usually involved the most ear-shattering chaos she could create. To end the racket and save her own eardrums, Sabrina vigorously shook Daphne until her eyes opened.

"Whazzamattawitalllthebangin?" Daphne grumbled.

"It's time to start the day," Granny said, finally setting down her pot and spoon.

The old woman was fully dressed, wearing a bulky coat, mittens, a scarf, and boots. She might have looked as if she were going whale hunting if not for her bright pink hat with a sunflower appliqué in its center. "We've got to get in a little escape training before everyone arrives."

Both girls groaned.

"Granny, we hate escape training. We're no good at it," Daphne complained.

"Nonsense," the old woman said, pulling back the blankets and helping the girls out of bed. "You're both very good at it."

"Then how come we've never escaped?" Sabrina grumbled.

Granny did her best to hide her smile, then turned to exit the room. "Get dressed, girls. There is no time for dillydallying."

"What should we wear?" Sabrina called after her.

"Something warm. Something very, very warm."

The girls had come to understand their grandmother well in the time they had been living with her. If she said to dress lightly, that meant wear as little as possible. If she said to bring a towel, that meant bring a dozen. If she said to dress warmly, that meant two pairs of long johns, four pairs of socks, heavy blue jeans, boots, two sweaters, scarves, mittens, and a down coat. "Very,

very warm" might well mean they should bring a portable space heater.

The girls helped each other into thick sweaters, heavy pants, and puffy coats. Sabrina added a wooden sword to her ensemble, shoving it into her belt. Puck had left it in the living room the night before and she had snatched it for her own.

"What's that for?" Daphne asked, eyeing the weapon.

"I'm tired of his surprises," Sabrina said. "This time I'm going to be ready."

Daphne nodded knowingly.

With mittens, scarves, and earmuffs in place, the girls stepped into the hall just as their uncle Jake opened the bathroom door. He was still in his pajamas and had a toothbrush hanging out of his mouth.

"Good luck," he said, giving them a thumbs-up.

"Easy for you to say," Sabrina mumbled. "You're not spending your morning running from a psychopath."

"You say that like it's not going to be any fun," Uncle Jake said with a wink, then he ducked back into the bathroom.

Granny was waiting for them in front of a door at the end of the hall. She unlocked it and led the girls inside.

The spare room remained locked because it contained three very valuable things: an ornate, full-length mirror and Sabrina's sleeping parents, Henry and Veronica Grimm. The trio's arrival didn't disturb their sleep in the least. It was deep and, unfortunately, enchanted. Nothing the family had tried could wake Henry and Veronica up. Sabrina was desperate to break the spell that kept them unconscious, but Granny's training sessions kept getting in the way.

The old woman buttoned her coat and turned to the mirror. "Mirror, mirror, the morning is blessed. We're here to train. Are you dressed?"

"Bright-eyed and bushy-tailed," Mirror said, appearing in the reflection. "Puck is ready for you. Sorry, girls, I tried to get some clues about what he has planned, but he was tight-lipped."

"Thanks for trying," Daphne said.

"The girls are not supposed to know what he's up to, Mirror. I'm trying to teach them how to prepare for the unpredictable."

"Well, you've chosen the right assistant in Puck," Mirror said.

"Shall we get started, girls?" Granny asked, nudging them toward the mirror.

Daphne stepped through the reflection and vanished.

"I hope there will be hot cocoa after this," Sabrina said to her grandmother with a grumble.

"I think I can arrange that," the old woman said. She took Sabrina's hand and together they stepped through the mirror, too.

Waiting for them was a short man in a black tuxedo.

"Good morning, Mirror," Sabrina said.

"Look at my little snow bunnies," Mirror said as he clapped his hands with glee. "Are you ready for your escape training?"

Daphne grumbled something under her breath.

"That's the spirit!" said Mirror, leading the group down the grand hallway.

He stopped at a door with a plaque that read THE SNOW QUEEN'S KINGDOM. Granny handed Mirror her keys, and he went to work unlocking the door.

"Wait a minute. There's an entire kingdom behind this door?" Sabrina asked.

"Indeed," Granny said. "The Snow Queen's homeland is under lock and key in the Hall of Wonders."

Mirror opened the door, and a bitter wind blasted the group. Sabrina swore she could feel icicles forming on her back teeth. She looked up at her grandmother. "Are you crazy?"

"This is going to be fun," the old woman said as she stepped inside.

"Good luck! I'll thaw you out when you get back," Mirror said as he nudged the girls through and closed the door.

## ABOUT THE AUTHOR

Michael Buckley is the *New York Times* bestselling author of the Sisters Grimm and NERDS series, *Kel Gilligan's Daredevil Stunt Show*, and the Undertow Trilogy. He has also written and developed television shows for many networks. Michael lives in Brooklyn, New York, with his wife, Alison; their son, Finn; and their dog, Friday.